# The Little Mouse

C W Lovatt

A Wild Wolf Publication

*Published by Wild Wolf Publishing in 2018*

*Copyright © 2018 C W Lovatt*

ISBN: 978-1-907954-67-2
Also available in E-Book Edition

www.wildwolfpublishing.com

*For Nanny, Iris, and Evie, (and Kai, and Jackson ... and anyone else who has yet to make an appearance)*

# Acknowledgements

Thanks go out to Rod Glenn and the rest of Wild Wolf Publishing for agreeing to take on a project that was about as far from my usual genre of Historical Fiction as you can get. Thanks also to the very talented Angel-Rose for the cover art and illustrations. I have a feeling that the world is going to see more of her work very soon. Thanks to Helen Cripps, Diana Milne, Elaine Routledge Taylor, Becky Williams and Faith Morrison for reading the original manuscripts, and their invaluable feedback. Special thanks to Diana Milne for her excellent work on the blurb.

Also special thanks to Helen Cripps for urging the story toward publication in the first place. Very special thanks go out to Helen's granddaughters: Iris Eyley, and Evie Peck, whose interest in my work was the catalyst required to get the wheels turning toward publication. Finally, last, but not least, all those wonderful people out there on social media, whose overwhelming show of support kept this project moving forward. Thank you all.

Once there was a little mouse who lived in a forest that bordered a great kingdom. Because he was the youngest, and therefore the tiniest, his mother named him 'Kit', which was as much a term of endearment as it was a real mouse name.

One day when he was just a wee mouse, Kit and his brothers, and sisters, and mother happened to be by the edge of the forest, feasting on pinecones. In the distance, he spied a great castle on a hill.

Scurrying over to his mother, he demanded to know the nature of the castle.

His mother, who was very wise, said, "That is the castle of the king of the land."

"What land is that, Mother?"

"My, but you are all questions this day, my son." She smiled, for previous to this, she had been besieged with 'Why was grass green?' and 'Why was the sky blue?' and 'Why was the sun warm?' and many other things, besides. Now, gesturing, she said, "All the land you see spread before you, all the green fields and vineyards, all the cattle, pigs, and sheep, and all of the people thereof, that expanse is the land and holdings of the king."

"It seems a very fine land," the little mouse noted.

"I suppose it is," his mother allowed. "I daresay the king is very wealthy."

The little mouse pondered this for a moment, then asked, "And this forest, Mother? Does the king rule over us here, in our forest?"

His mother smiled warmly. This son of hers was the smallest and youngest of her brood, but he asked such questions! This was good, she knew, because his mind was young and eager to be filled.

"No, my son. Our forest is free. It belongs to none but ourselves and the other creatures who dwell here."

"What is 'free'?"

The good dame hesitated. She knew that her little mouse had asked a very important question, and she wanted to answer correctly. She thought, and thought, but the best she could do was to say, "Freedom is the most important thing to all the creatures of the forest. We go where we will, and do as we like, as best we may. That is freedom."

Now the young mouse thought, and thought.

He was just a little mouse, and could not yet go where he wanted, or do what he liked.

These were things that his mother would not yet allow. She had made freedom sound wonderful, but he wasn't sure if it was something that pertained to himself.

So he asked, "Am I free, Mother?"

Goodness! How one question led to another with this, her youngest and tiniest.

"You are my baby," she laughed, touching the tip of her nose to his own tiny black one, "and that is even better!"

"But …"

"Enough, my inquisitive son!" she laughed, rolling him over, and over until he giggled. "Give your mother some rest from all of these endless questions, and instead, go and play with your brothers and sisters. You will understand more when you are older."

So the wee fellow did as his mother bade him, and soon enough, forgot about freedom, and the castle, and the Great Kingdom while he played rough and tumble games with his siblings.

So it was that this was the way it stayed for

quite some time, until the day of the Great Fire.

Things might have been much worse, if their mother hadn't smelled the smoke on the wind and knew what it meant. She had seen fire before, and knew that it was to be feared.

"Come children!" she cried.

Just then Orso, the bear, charged past their home, amongst the roots of the great old oak tree. Kit thought that he had never seen Orso in such a hurry, and he *knew* that he had never seen him afraid the way that he was now – wide-eyed, and grunting in terror, looking neither to left nor right, as he careened headlong to the river.

The young mice huddled around their mother, infected by her fear. She too, led them in the direction Orso had gone – toward the river.

Several other creatures of the forest passed them as they went. Rowena, the doe, with her young spotted fawn, Chaser, at her heels; Tod, the fox, appeared, but before the young mice could even squeak with fright, he was by them in a flash, his bushy tail low and straight behind him. Little mice were, apparently, the last thing on his mind this day.

Likewise, grumpy old Gort, the badger, waddled along, discontentedly, on his short, stumpy legs, without pause following his nose to the river. Then there was Bumper, the hare; Lulu, the skunk; Amos, the porcupine, and a host of others, racing by so fast that they were mere flitting shadows before they were gone.

Behind them, the little mouse could hear a mighty roar, and crackling. A great, hot wind blew so hard that he felt that it must pick him up, and carry him away.

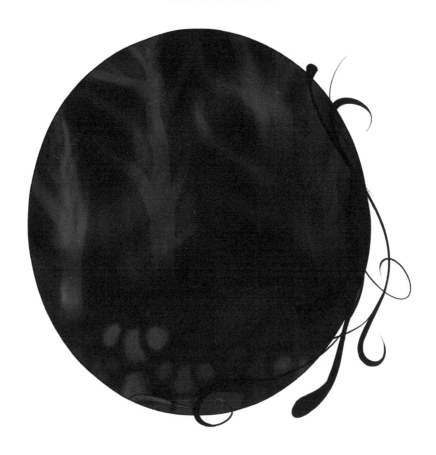

"Hurry, children!" his mother cried. "We must beat the flames to the river!"

Kit glanced over his shoulder, too curious not to want to see what they were fleeing, and saw that the forest was a vast curtain of angry fire. Even as he watched, a great pine tree burst into flame, sending exploding, fiery cones in every direction. One landed beside the path in front of him. Immediately flames began to lick into the tinder-dry undergrowth, curling the brown grass to black in the twinkle of an eye.

The little mouse squeaked, put his head down, and charged past his mother. Whoever was going to be last to the river, it wasn't going to be him.

They reached the water's edge just as the willows on the shore began to go up with a 'woof'.

None of the mice hesitated, but flung themselves into the water, incredibly fortunate that it happened to be a shallow eddy, free of strong current, or jackfish. They huddled in the water with the other creatures, sometimes with no more than the tips of their noses above the surface while the conflagration raged all around them.

All of that day they stayed there, and all of that night, as well. As the fire raged and waned, at times the shallow water seemed almost too hot to bear. Other times, the wind blew smoke down to the surface, making them all choke and cough. The one constant were the flames – great sheets of crimson, raging all around, reflecting off the river, until everything in the whole wide world glowed an angry red.

All of this Kit saw through little apple seed eyes of terror. Until he had seen his home destroyed, he had not known what fire was, and now it was his entire world.

He had joined his brothers and sisters huddled around their mother. Some had their eyes tightly shut against the horror, others were wide-eyed with fright, and though they wanted to, could not seem to be able to close them to what that they were forced to witness.

A combination of exhaustion and fear can often play tricks on the mind. Sometimes it may trigger hallucinations.

Sometimes it will even cause dreams; and unbelievable as it sounds, sometime during that horrible night, the little mouse thought that he had fallen asleep, for he was dreaming that the Great Mouse was speaking to him.

"Little mouse, do not be afraid," He said, in a voice that was kind, and as old as the hills.

Kit's exhausted mind was confused: if this was a dream, why could he still see his brothers and sisters huddled around his mother, and the raging fire beyond?

Why could he feel the heat of the flames on the tip of his nose?

"But Lord," he trembled, "I can't help it, I *am* afraid."

"There is no need," said the voice from somewhere in his mind, "for I have great plans for you."

"But what of my mother, and brothers and sisters," asked this selfless little mouse, "will we all be saved?"

"You will all be saved."

"But our home is gone. It has been destroyed by the fire."

The Great Mouse was silent.

"Why, Lord?" the little mouse asked through little tears, "Why has this happened?"

"Because I have chosen you."

"Chosen me?" Kit asked, bewildered, "Chosen me for what?"

Just then a great wind arose that was like no other. It fanned the flames on the mightiest of the burning trees, sending a single finger of God-Fire high up into the sky before bending it back to earth, lancing through the night, plunging straight towards the family of mice huddled by the river's edge.

The little mouse was aware of being seized in cold flame, hot wind, blasting earth, and the cauldron of the river's water. He felt it swarm over, around, and through his body, and sear his mind.

He felt it go to such depths inside him that he was surprised that chasms so deep could be found in one so tiny.

At first he was so terrified that he thought that his heart would burst; but as time went by, and he felt no pain, he realized that this must be all part of his dream.

Sure enough, as suddenly as it had started, the earth, wind and fire were gone, and, with them, the Great Mouse as well. Dazed, Kit checked his body all over to see where he had been burnt, but there were no signs.

What was even more curious, none of the others seemed to have noticed that great finger of flame. Anything so powerful would surely have caused some remark, but no one even asked him if he had been scorched.

Finally, exhausted, he *did* fall into a deep sleep...and did not dream at all.

.    .    .

B y the next morning, the flames had raged themselves into oblivion, as all that could be destroyed had been consumed. Here and there, stumps and boles of trees still crackled, and smoked threateningly, but their mother deemed it safe enough for them to leave the water.

After so long in the river, they were very hungry, and were in desperate need of food; but the fire had laid waste to the forest, leaving a barren land in its wake, covered in ash. Much searching, provided them with some seeds and pinecones, but these were few and far between. All the mice were dazed by the harrowing experience, and exhausted, as well, but there was little time to rest, for food was the first necessity, and there never seemed to be enough.

His dream long forgotten, it was at the end of the second day, with his empty tummy rumbling, that the little mouse recalled the rich kingdom at the edge of where the forest had been. His gnawing hunger was such that, right then and there, he made up his mind

Turning to his mother, he said, "I will go to the Great Kingdom, and make my fortune. Then I will come back with food for us all."

His good mother recoiled in dismay at such a foolish notion. She tried to convince him to stay, and not to venture into that dangerous, foreign land. She tried to convince him that the family must remain together, she tried everything she could think of to make him change his mind, but she saw that he would not be swayed. Perhaps, deep in her heart, she had already sensed that this day would come, so she bowed her head in sad acceptance.

"My son, you are no longer a child. The world is spread out before you. Go where you will, but I beg of you, never forget your family, or," she said, tears welling in her dear little eyes, "your poor old mother."

Kit promised solemnly that he would never forget.

"Come back to me safe, and sound." She hugged him close and hard before finally letting him go. All his brothers and sisters hugged him as well, for they too were sad that he was leaving.

Then, with all goodbyes said, and all hugs hugged, with a final wave, the little mouse, turned, and began to make his way through the ashes of the forest, on his way to the land of the Great Kingdom.

.    .    .

The world is a dangerous place for a little mouse, and all the more so if the grass and brush has been burnt away, leaving no place to hide.

Sure enough, after no more than an hour or two along the way, he was spied by Tod's keen and hungry eye. The fox leapt to block the way, teeth bared, saliva drooling.

Kit knew that there was no place to run for cover, so stood his ground. It seemed that before it had begun, his quest was ending in doom. Still, if doom it was to be, he was determined to meet his fate bravely.

"Ho! Little mouse," Tod growled, hungrily, "I have not eaten since the fire. I am famished, and so I am going to eat you."

The little mouse drew himself to his full, inconsiderable height. Frantically, his mind raced, trying to think of a way out of this dangerous situation. He could not run, and he could see by the hungry and desperate look in Tod's eyes, that he would not answer to pleading, either.

Unable to think of anything else, he cried bravely, "No, Tod, you will not eat me!"

Tod, who had been about to pounce on his helpless victim, stopped short, both amused and surprised.

"Not eat you?" He laughed, but without much humour, "And why, pray, should I not eat you? You are but a little mouse, after all, and I am a hungry fox."

In desperation, Kit stared hard with his little eyes directly into Tod's famished ones.

Then something strange and wonderful happened – he remembered his dream.

Suddenly he felt the power of Earth, Wind, Fire and Water surging up from the deep chasms inside of his being. It came so suddenly, and with such strength, that he felt it burst from his own tiny little eyes, straight into Tod's great round ones.

"No, Tod," he said in a low, threatening voice. "I am really a very big mouse, with long, sharp teeth."

Silence hung suspended between the fox and the mouse. Tod felt the power that came from the little mouse's eyes … and he began to feel his will fade away.

"Of course," he agreed, "you are a very large mouse, with long, sharp teeth."

Kit was very surprised to hear the fox say this, but he didn't dare let it show.

"And you will not eat me" he said.

"Eat you?" Tod laughed at what now seemed to him to be a not-so-funny joke. "No, of course I won't eat you. That would be ridiculous, because you are a very large mouse with very large …"

"And dangerous," the little mouse interjected.

"… and dangerous teeth," Tod agreed.

Then the fox appeared to be nervous, and frightened, because such a large mouse with such long, dangerous teeth might eat *him*, instead. He turned, and would have run away with his bushy tail between his legs, but Kit had an idea, and took pity on him.

"Wait," he cried, and the fox hesitated, darting a worried look over his shoulder.

"I am going to the Great Kingdom by the edge of the forest," he said, "There I will make my fortune, and bring back food for my family." Thinking quickly, he added, "No creature should be afraid of another during this time. We should all be friends, instead."

"Yes," Tod agreed, instantly. "We *should* be friends."

"You must come with me to the Great Kingdom. Together, we will bring back food for everyone in the forest."

"Oh large mouse, with long, sharp, dangerous teeth," the fox cried, "that is a very good idea. I will come with you!" So the two set off together on their journey to the Great Kingdom.

By and by, they came upon Gort. The badger's long snout was snuffling grumpily amongst the ashes, searching for food.

Tod and the little mouse were quite close before Gort's near-sighted eyes told him that there was someone close at hand.

"What? Who's there?" he growled suspiciously, thrusting out his snout for a snarly sniff, "Oh, it's you, Tod," he grumbled in great ill temper. "Go away, and leave me alone. I haven't any time for foxes today." Then scarcely were the words out, than he exclaimed, "What's this? I smell a little mouse!" He peered down the length of his nose, and sure enough, there was Kit. "Ah ha!" he cried, "Little mouse, you will not make much of a meal, but I have not eaten all day, and I am very hungry."

The little mouse still felt the power of Earth, Wind, Fire, and Water, and was no longer afraid. He hopped audaciously onto the badgers snout, and scampered up so that Gort could see him clearly.

Staring hard into the badger's eyes, he said, "No Gort, you are not hungry at all. Why, don't you remember? You just had a wonderful meal only a minute ago."

Gort's head tilted to one side, uncertainly.

"A meal?"

"Yes," said Kit, "A very wonderful meal. You couldn't eat another bite. Don't you remember?"

"Yeeeesss," Gort began slowly, but then brightened as the memory returned. "Yes! A wonderful meal, just as you say, little mouse."

"He's not a little mouse," Tod corrected the badger. "He's actually a very large mouse with long, sharp, dangerous teeth."

"You don't say?" Gort said, in a sort of wonder.

"Yes," said the little mouse, "and Tod and I are on our way to the Great Kingdom to make our fortune, and bring back food for all of the creatures in the forest. You must come along with us."

"Come along with you? To the Great Kingdom?" Gort's wits were somewhat slower than the fox's.

"Yes," Kit reaffirmed, "to the Great Kingdom. And," he added, "instead of being grumpy all of the time, you must be happy."

The badger's brow wrinkled doubtfully.

"Happy? Me?" and then, "*All* the time?"

"Yes, *all* the time."

"Oh."

Gort pondered this imponderable for a moment, and then stretched his lips up from his snout in a dreadful smile.

"Howsh thish?" he asked through his fangs.

Tod took a nervous step backwards, but the little mouse said, "That will do nicely, thank you. Now, come along, we must be on our way to the Great Kingdom. There's not a moment to lose."

So, the three unlikely friends hurried on their way. Presently, Rowena and Chaser were spied in the distance.

As the trio neared, the deer, although with little to fear from a badger or a fox - and none at all from a little mouse - skittered nervously. The fire had left them without food or shelter, and they knew that it was dangerous to be abroad. Finally, however, with Kit shouting at the top of his lungs, he was able to draw them nearer.

Chaser was the first to approach, stretching his neck out and down until his nose was almost touching that of the little mouse.

"Look Momma," he said, in a high, sweet voice, "it's a little mouse."

"He's not," said Tod, "he's actually a very large mouse with long, sharp, dangerous teeth."

"I'b vewy happy!" Gort burbled, through horribly grinning jaws.

"Yes," said Kit, staring intently into their eyes, "and we are going to the Great Kingdom, that lies on the edge of the forest. There we will make our fortunes, and bring back food for everyone. You must come along with us." Then he added reassuringly, "We are all friends here."

"Okay!" Chaser agreed instantly.

"The Great Kingdom?" Rowena asked in a

dream-like voice. "Yes, all right, but we're so hungry."

"You have just had your fill from that fine meadow over yonder," the little mouse said, pointing, "and you couldn't possibly hold another bite."

Rowena and Chaser both looked to where Kit had indicated, and sure enough, through hypnotized eyes, they saw a great green meadow of tall, sweet grass.

"Yes," Rowena agreed, "you are right. How silly of me to forget."

So the three became five.

Not much later, Amos could be seen making his way towards them, his lumbering walk swaying his body back and forth like a bush in the wind. But as soon as he saw the badger and the fox, he curled up into a ball, and rattled a warning with his quills.

The little mouse asked the others to wait while he scurried up to the frightened porcupine.

"It's all right, Amos," he said.

"Who's there?" Amos' voice came muffled from somewhere within the bristling ball of quills.

Kit whispered in a very tiny, harmless, little voice, "No one you need fear."

After a moment, the mountain of quills shuffled just enough for half of one eye to peep out.

"Why," he said, "you're just a little mouse."

"He's actually a very *large* mouse, with long, sharp, dangerous teeth."

"I'b vewy happy!"

"We are all friends!"

"Yes," the little mouse said, agreeing with Rowena and Chaser, "and we're all off to the Great Kingdom that lies on the edge of the forest. There we will make our fortunes, and bring back food for everyone. You must come along with us."

"Oh?"

"Yes," said Kit, "and you must not be bashful."

"All right," Amos said, uncurling. He smiled timidly at the little mouse, and his companions. They all smiled reassuringly back at him, even Gort … sort of.

So the five became six.

Over the very next rise, they came face to face with Bumper.

The hare gave a start, and was already several yards away before being brought up short when everyone cried, "Wait!"

Bumper stopped, but when he saw Tod, he hopped a short distance further before stopping again, and turning, suspicion etched on every line of his face. "What do you want?" he asked.

All six chimed in.

"We're on our way – he's actually a very large mouse – I'b vewy happy – to the Great Kingdom that lies – with very long, sharp – we're all friends – at the edge of the forest – dangerous teeth – I'm not bashful – and you must come with us."

Bumper thought this was the strangest thing he had ever heard.

"The Great Kingdom has many man-creatures," he said, "and is very dangerous."

Kit crept forward, away from the others. He looked deep into Bumper's eyes.

"Perhaps not," he said.

After a minute, Bumper agreed. "No, perhaps not."

So, the six became seven.

Around the next bend, having heard the commotion, Lulu waited, shivering with fright. Her tail was raised and fanned – the posture that skunks assume just before they spray.

Five of the six turned to flee.

"Wait!" the little mouse cried.

His friends stopped, but would come no closer.

Kit scampered around to where he could speak to Lulu, face to face.

"Don't be afraid," he said.

"I'm not afraid," Lulu trembled in a quavering voice.

"My friends and I are off to the Great Kingdom that lies on the edge of the forest," said the little mouse, "and we want you to come with us."

Lulu looked timidly at Kit's friends. She wasn't very reassured by the way that they looked back at her.

"They don't want me," she said, "because I smell so bad."

"How can you say that?" the little mouse asked. He looked deep into her eyes, and said,

"You smell wonderful ... when you're not afraid." Then he turned to his companions, studying each of them intently, "Doesn't she?"

They thought for a moment, and then all agreed that she did, indeed, have a lovely smell ... when she wasn't afraid.

"So, you must never be afraid," Rowena said. "We are all friends here."

"I'b *vewy* happy to meet you," said Gort, trying his best to smile warmly.

"Me too." Amos smiled unabashedly.

Tod and Chaser came up to touch noses with Lulu, and then, eventually, so did everyone.

So, the seven became eight.

The day wore on, and they were almost to the charred remnants of the edge of the forest, when the great, lumbering, brown, shaggy form of Orso hove into sight.

As they drew nearer, the eight companions could see that something was wrong with the huge bear. He seemed to be wandering haphazardly here and there, pausing every other step to shake his head, and try to reach a spot that was too far up the hump on his back.

As they got even closer, they could hear him moaning plaintively, seeking to ease some sort of torment.

Poor Orso, even though he had lain as low as he could out in the middle of the river, the shallow summer water had not been deep enough to cover him completely, and his back had been burned and singed in numerous places.

His pain was such that he had no thoughts of food, but instead, maddened by his suffering, he was trying physically to dig it out with his claws. However, he could not reach those places where his fur was singed and burnt away, and his skin black and blistered.

This became obvious to the others when they had drawn close enough to see the ugly scars that the fire had left. All but Kit came no nearer. A bear was dangerous enough, but to come close to one maddened by pain was suicide.

Orso was not in his right mind. All he knew was that he hurt, and sought to destroy whatever was causing that hurt. Should any other creature come across his path, he would think that this was the cause of his misfortune, and charge.

However, if the little mouse was afraid, he kept it well hidden. In fact, he never hesitated, but scampered up to the great bear until he was lost in his shadow.

"G-R-R-R-R-R! UFF! UFF!" Orso groaned. "Stop! Stop! Get out of me! Go away! You are not Roots and Honey! You are Bad and Hurt! Go away, or I will bite, and bite!"

He was not speaking to Kit, for he had yet to notice him. Instead, he was growling at his pain, in the way of his kind.

"I'll bite you! I'll bite you! I'll tear you apart with my claws! You are not Roots and Honey! You are Bad Things! Go away! Go away!"

He made another ineffectual swipe at his back with a fearsomely clawed forepaw, and shook his head to try to clear the fog of his suffering away.

All the while, the little mouse had been trying to get the great bear's attention, but Orso - near-sighted as he was, and preoccupied with his agony as he was – would have lumbered on past, unseeing. So Kit knew that there was nothing else he could do but scramble up the bear's hind leg, clinging to the dense, brown fur, until he was atop of that great, shaggy back.

Here, even the little mouse paused. The scars of Orso's wounds were fearsome to behold. Great blisters of raw flesh, surrounded by blackened skin and charred, evil-smelling fur, barred his path.

Kit was shocked, and horrified to think that the bear should endure such great pain, and his heart went out to him.

Earth, Wind, Fire, and Water formed in his mind, whirling in a tornado of the elements – surging its power through, over, and around him. A colossus of Power – a world of strong magic – stars in the noon-day sky – an incredibly old mouse, with incredibly kind and gentle eyes, his face filling the sky, looking down from a vast height, and speaking to him. All the while, there was the Earth, Wind, Fire, and Water; the Water … the Water … yes, and the Earth and the Wind. The little mouse concentrated on these the way the kind old mouse had bid him to, and poured his mind into the dreadful wounds that were not Roots and Honey.

When Kit finally came back to himself, he was

still in a daze ... and the charred, ugly, evil-smelling patches on Orso's back were beginning to heal.

Even as he watched, the raw red flesh turned a healthy pink as benign skin healed and stitched, replacing the ugly welts and lesions.

"Ahhh! Roots and Honey!" Orso sighed, just moments before flinging himself onto his back.

The little mouse had to leap for his life to prevent himself from being crushed under the brute's tremendous weight. He landed in a pile of ash, and began to sneeze.

"Ahhhh!" Orso sighed mightily, and writhed, grinding his back into the earth. "Itchy-itch!"

Having cleared the ash from his nose, Kit tried again to get the bear's attention, but Orso was having none of it.

He continued to writhe and grind, happily baring large swathes of ground, all the while muttering sighs of "Itchy-itch!" intermittently with thankful gasps of "Roots and Honey!" until he, and anyone near him, was covered in ash. Naturally, this started the little mouse sneezing all over again.

At last, his eyes closed in ecstatic relief, Orso gave one last, great writhe before rolling over on his side, and promptly dropped off to sleep.

Frustrated, Kit scampered up to the bear, trying to waken him, but instead, was bowled over by a windy breath when he began to snore. He tried everything. He tried scurrying up to an ear and shouting, and barely escaped being crushed again, this time by an irritated paw. He tried to lift one of the great eyelids, but it was too heavy. He tried tickling his nose, but this only caused the bear to sneeze, in turn causing Kit to be blown away several feet to land in a wet and dishevelled heap.

Finally, defeated, he stood before the bear, riddled with indecision. Then, without any other option available, he lay down ... and waited.

One by one, timidly at first, the others crept closer, too.

First Tod stepped daintily up to the monster, ready at a moment's notice to take flight. Carefully, he sniffed at the great snout, and sneezed violently, before sitting down by the little mouse. Then, like the mouse, he too lay down, resting his head on his paws.

Then came Gort, happily suspicious at first, and then just happy, before taking his place beside Tod.

Next came Amos, unbashful, then sweet-smelling Lulu. Finally Bumper, Rowena and Chaser came closer, but stopped a safe distance away.

Then all of them lay down, and all of them curled up, and were soon fast asleep.

The afternoon dimmed to evening. As the first stars appeared in the eastern sky, the evening surrendered to the stillness of the night, broken intermittently by a snore or a murmur as someone stirred in a dream.

Off in the distance came the hoot of an owl.

.　　.　　.

The next morning saw everyone awake, and waiting expectantly for Orso to join the new day; but the bear had suffered greatly, and lost much energy. So it wasn't until the sun had climbed high into the sky before one bleary, blood-shot eye flickered open briefly, saw the company gathered around him, and then closed again. A minute went by before it flickered open again … then closed again … open … then closed … opened … then closed …

Suddenly, there was a mighty bellow, and Orso was on his feet, lunging straight for Rowena.

"R-R-R-R-R-R-R!! Hungry!" he roared. "Roots and Honey! No food since fire! Orso *hungry*! R-R-R-R-R-R-R!!"

Had Rowena and Chaser been as close as the others, one of them would almost certainly have met an untimely end. As it was, the startled deer bounded away in the nick of time. The fearsome sweep of Orso's great claws narrowly missed Chaser, but came so close that they scythed hairs from his dun-coloured coat.

Finding his charge frustrated, Orso swung around in a wide, lumbering arc, preparing to renew the chase, when he noticed that there was a little mouse, hanging on for dear life to his snout.

Forgetting all about breakfast for the moment, he ground to a stop, exclaiming, "Huh? A l'il mousey!"

Kit stared deeply into one of his eyes.

"You are *not* hungry, Orso," he said. "See?"

Orso turned to look where he was bidden, and saw a beautiful glade filled with flowers, and absolutely aswarm with bees. Dozens of branches of the surrounding trees were bent double with fat hives, each one of them heavy with honey. Of course, he had just eaten his fill – eaten to bursting, in fact. How, he wondered, had he ever thought that he could be hungry?

"Uh … dunno," he shrugged, and then grinned widely, his eyes crossing as he regarded the creature on his nose, "Hi, l'il mousey!"

"Ahem," Tod began, "Actually, sir, he's a quite *big* mouse with …"

"A large, *friendly* mouse," the little mouse interrupted, "isn't that right, Tod?"

Kit knew that having a frightened Orso running amok would be almost as bad as a hungry one.

"Yes, of course," Tod agreed, "A large, friendly mouse." Wasn't that what he had just been about to say?

"Hello," Gort smiled, and Orso took an uncertain step back.

"Don't be frightened," the little mouse said, "He's just happy."

"I'b *vewy* happy," the badger agreed.

"We're all friends here," Rowena and Chaser chimed … still from a safe distance.

"Hi there," Amos beamed forthrightly, "I'm not bashful."

"I'm not afraid," Lulu said, then shyly "You can smell me, if you like."

"We're going to the Great Kingdom," Bumper explained. "Perhaps it won't be dangerous."

"And we want you to come with us," finished Kit.

Orso thought, and thought.

"Da Great Kingdom?"

His massive head swivelled around to look out upon the rich lowlands spread before them. In the midst of the verdant green fields, a postage-stamp castle perched high atop a postage-stamp hill.

Once more, Orso's eyes crossed onto the mouse.

Hopefully, he asked, "Roots and Honey?"

"Yes Orso," the little mouse promised. "Roots and Honey."

The great bear's happy grin grew immensely wide, and dream-like.

"Okie-dokie!"

Thus the eight became nine.

.  .  .

By the time they came to the farm, their illusion of being full was wearing thin.

Bellies were rumbling, Gort's smile had reverted to its normal saturnine state, and everyone agreed that it was an improvement.

Bumper was becoming more nervous, in fact, they were all becoming more nervous the further they travelled into this strange land. For of course, none had ventured this far before, and the fear of the unknown hung over the little party like a dark cloud.

Even Kit was feeling uneasy.

This is where his freedom had brought him – leading this unlikely group into a strange land, inhabited by strange creatures, who, if the legends were to be believed, might well react with hostility. Why had he gone to so much trouble to bring his companions along? He had to admit that he'd compelled them – that there had been no freedom in their choice to follow. What of that?

At first he had thought that it was mere survival that had caused him to invade their minds with his new power, and convince them to come along; after all, it was far more preferable than being made into a meal. However, he could have simply asked them go their own way and leave him in peace, but he hadn't. In fact, he had gone out of his way to bring along every creature that had crossed his path. Why?

For all that freedom was, he wasn't sure if he ever had been free, but instead, was acting on some will other than his own. He felt compelled, and in turn, compelled others, ever deeper into the unknown, towards the castle that was looming larger with every step. He felt that his decisions were no more his own than were those of his companions.

They had travelled in silence, and as the day wore on, he had tried to conjure thoughts of Earth, Wind, Fire, and Water. He had sent out silent entreaties to the Great Mouse, and listened carefully, through the tramping and shuffling feet of the others for a reply, but no vision or voice came to him. He felt alone and unsure. Worse, he could feel the effects of his magic beginning to wear off the others, and he wondered what form of madness had brought him here in the first place?

These were compelling questions that required much thought, but when Kit's nose detected a wondrously sweet scent wafting on the breeze, they vanished into thin air. Looking around, he saw that the others had noticed the same wonderful smell, too, and, with his questions now forgotten, the little mouse soon found it difficult to keep up as the pace began to quicken.

"Y-U-U-M-M-M-M!" Orso groaned, after he had paused, nose testing the air. Then he put his head down, and began to lumber forward with a purpose.

In short order, one by one, as each caught the scent, everyone started off after the bear, leaving Kit to follow as best he could.

"Wait!" he cried, but in vain. Even Amos was making better headway, and seemed unaware of anything else but following his nose.

"Wait," the little mouse cried again, "No, we mustn't." He wasn't sure why, but he knew something was wrong.

He tried to hurry, but he was just a little mouse, and his strength wasn't what it should have been. He hadn't eaten for some time, and it was starting to tell. By the time that he arrived at the garden just outside of the little yard - that held the little, thatched cottage and some, scattered outbuildings - he knew that he was too late.

Orso was sitting upright, legs spread amongst a row of green, leafy tops. His head was down, brow creased with concentration, while he dug through the rich earth with his fore-claws. Then, grunting with pleasure, he popped out a turnip, and happily began to feed.

"Yummmm!" he said amidst much lip smacking, "Roots and Honey, but this is good!"

He finished the turnip in two bites, and promptly busied himself by digging up another half-dozen in double-quick order.

"Orso, no!" Kit pleaded, but the great bear seemed in a world of his own, and was not even aware that he was being spoken to.

Over in a lettuce patch, Rowena, Chaser and Bumper were delicately nibbling the fresh green leaves with obvious pleasure. Already Bumper's girth had expanded noticeably, but he showed no signs of slowing down.

The little mouse saw Amos rooting over by a

carrot patch, and like the others, seemed too preoccupied to pay attention to anything other than this windfall.

Kit ran amongst them, pleading, and warning, but he might as well not have existed for all the effect he had.

Something was dreadfully wrong, but every time he tried to fasten his mind on what it was, it would flit away from his grasp like an elusive butterfly.

Then a sudden, startled cackling – abruptly cut short - gave him a hint.

Here and there, about the yard, fat, white bird-like creatures were busily pecking at food scattered on the ground. Until now, the little mouse had been too preoccupied to notice them. Apparently, Tod, Gort and Lulu had not.

The fat birds must have been the scent that they were following all along. No doubt, they had walked straight through the vegetable garden without even noticing it, and made straight for their prey.

Even as Kit watched, Tod seized one of the birds by the neck. At the same instant, Gort fastened his teeth on a leg.

"Oh dear!" said Kit to no one in particular, and scampered as hard as he could up to the yard, but he was already too late.

After a short tug-of-war, Tod released his hold on the bird, as there were plenty to go around. He had just succeeded in capturing a wildly squawking second one, when the yard erupted in an explosion of noise.

"R-R-ROWF! ROWF! ROWF!" Filled with teeth and bad temper, a great wolf-like creature burst around the corner of the cottage, and was lunging towards Tod … who stood paralyzed with surprise.

"Dirty, chicken-stealing fox!" the wolf-like creature snarled, "I'll bite you! I'll bite you, and tear you to pieces!"

There could have been no doubt that he would have done just that, were it not for the chain fastened to the collar around the beast's neck.

It had been so intent on causing the promised dismemberment to the fox, that the wolf-like creature had apparently forgotten it was there, himself. In fact, he was in mid-leap when he and his savage baying were brought up short with a startled yelp. His body was swung violently around before hitting the ground in a stunned heap, where it did not move.

The mouse arrived in the yard just as the door to the cottage swung open.

A large, burly man-creature stood on the front step. Like the wolf-creature, he seemed ill tempered. Unlike the wolf-creature, he carried a cudgel in one massive fist, and a heavy spear in the other.

At the back of Kit's mind, he realised that the legends were true. None of them had ever seen a chicken, or a dog, or a man before, but they recognised them from stories they'd all heard from their youth.

In fact, since time out of mind, frightening stories of dogs and men were used by many mothers throughout the forest to keep their children from straying too far from home; and now Kit saw that this was for good reason.

However, what was happening at the back of his mind went largely unnoticed, because the little mouse was too busy dealing with what was in the *front* of his mind, and, for that matter, in front of his eyes.

How were they ever going to escape from this mess?

"Bejayzuz!" quoth the man. He had spied Tod standing frozen with surprise. The chicken lay at his feet where he had dropped it at the dog's first baying. "A fox!" Then in stupefied fury, he shouted, "And a badger!"

For now he had seen Gort who still stood, likewise frozen with surprise, with his forepaw resting possessively on his own chicken.

Then, movement in the garden caused him to notice Orso, Rowena, and Chaser, as well.

The man's eyes widened with incredulity. "What the ...!"

When Tod broke to run away, the man likewise sprang into action. In one lightning motion, he flung the cudgel, clipping the fox painfully on his flank.

Tod shrieked, and staggered, but continued to flee. However, the cudgel must have done some damage, because one hind leg was now trailing uselessly behind him.

By now, Gort had taken flight, as well; but badgers aren't known for speed, and his short legs could scarcely keep up with the fox, lame as he was.

"Here, Brutus!" the man shouted.

The dog had since recovered from his near choking, and now his barking was once more joining in the general fray. The man unhooked his chain. "I've slowed the one for you, boy. The other you should be able to catch without too much trouble, I should think."

Brutus was off, straight as a hurled javelin, but the man scarcely noticed. "Now for that great brute, yonder," he said, grabbing the heavy spear more firmly, and was racing across the yard, into the garden.

Everything was happening so fast, and seemed to be completely out of control. Still, Kit had to try.

"No!" he squeaked, but no one heard him.

Then, in desperation, as the man raced by, he leapt onto a leg, and clung on for dear life.

The man, who was wearing nothing but a kilt-like garment, of course felt the mouse clinging to his shin. It was a day for incredible things, no doubt about it.

He shouted an oath, and kicked violently. The little mouse couldn't hold on, so was sent cartwheeling through the air. He landed heavily on the ground, and lay winded where he fell.

Meanwhile, Lulu had taken flight at Brutus' first baying. She had been in the act of raiding a hen's nest for eggs when the commotion started, so had escaped detection. Now the crops in the garden protected her as she made her way back the way that she had come. Unfortunately, this was also the route that Tod and Gort (with Brutus hotly pursuing) had chosen.

The fox and the badger – one maimed, the other slowed by nature – were doing their best to escape, but Brutus was like lightning, and would be upon Tod in a few more bounds.

Brutus was a wise dog, and a veteran at protecting the farm. First the fox, he reckoned. A quick shake ought to do the job, and that should leave ample time to deal with the badger.

He knew that badgers could be a handful, but if this one could be caught out in the open, he had no doubt that he was more than its match.

It was a good plan, as far as it went, but what Brutus hadn't counted on was Lulu.

He had just burst through a row of corn, baying triumphantly, when he found himself almost on top of a bushy black tail, raised and shaking, and all of the senses of his world were suddenly filled with the most appalling stench.

Lulu had connected in a way that she had

never connected before. Her spray had gone directly into Brutus' face, filling his eyes, ears, mouth and worst of all, his nose with her less than pretty smell. For Lulu was very frightened, indeed.

For the second time, the hound tried to yelp his surprise, and for the second time, wasn't able to. Instead, he retched, and gagged. Then he threw up. He tried to get his breath back, but whenever he inhaled, he was overwhelmed by that disgusting smell.

It stung his eyes, making it impossible to see; likewise, of course, it was impossible to *breathe* anything other than that dreadful spray. In frantic desperation, he ploughed his face into the ground, digging great furrows through the soft soil with his nose, again … and again … and again.

The man may have noticed this from the corner of his eye, and realised that all was not going as well as it might have, but like the little mouse, he had more important things on his mind.

Although it could be supposed that he was a brave man for taking on a bear with nothing but a spear, all he knew was that his crops were being destroyed, and the beast had to be stopped.

Meanwhile, after one startled, short-sighted look, when Brutus first rang out his challenge, Orso paid no more attention to what was happening around him. At that moment, in his world there were only turnips, turnips, and more turnips.

Like the others, he had never seen a man before. Unlike the others, he had still not seen a man, and didn't know enough to be afraid.

"Haw!" The man shouted at the same time he drove the spear deep into the bear's side.

Suddenly, pain and outrage invaded Orso's contented world. He might have run, but outside of fire, there was nothing that he feared, and now was no exception. When he reared up on his hind legs, and saw his puny adversary, there was still no reason for fear, only rage that hurt had been inflicted upon him.

"G-R-R-R-O-A-R-R-R-R!! You *bad*! I bite and I claw, and I – growf! – I tear you to pieces!"

"I'll kill ye, ye cursed bear!" The man roared his own hate-filled challenge, and struck again.

The blade of the spear glanced off a rib, and so

missed the great heart; but still, it bit deep, nicking an artery.

Orso swung a heavily clawed paw, but the man was agile, and dodged the blow before leaping in for the kill.

Up until this point, Amos had taken no part in the commotion. When it had started, he did not run, nor did he hide. What he did, true to his kind, was to curl into a ball, and hope that he was going to be left alone.

The man had been too preoccupied with his battle with Orso to notice the warning sound of rattling quills, but each time after the man had struck, he had retreated – with Orso following – until they had reached the carrot patch. So after he made his final lunge, the man unwittingly leapt back too close, and Amos' nerves, now stretched past all endurance, caused him to strike.

Once, twice, three times his tail slapped into the man's naked legs, embedding quills by the score with every blow.

The man shrieked, stumbled, and now screaming in terror, he fell.

Orso, mightily outraged by his pain, and

seeing his adversary helpless on the ground, lunged down to finish him.

"ORSO, NO!"

Earth, Wind, Fire, and Water coursed and whirled and raged within Kit as it never had before. His was no longer a mouse's tiny squeak, but, instead, a god's violent thunder. The earth rumbled, and shook, echoing through the hills.

It was such a commanding, mighty voice that it distracted the enraged bear. Although it was for the merest of seconds, it was enough.

"GROWF! OWF! OWF! I bite him! I tear him to pieces!"

"NO!" The commanding voice would brook no dissension.

Orso shook himself angrily, unused to holding his passions in check.

"But mousey! He hurt-hurt, big deep! I bite! I …"

Kit stood between him and the man. He shook his head and said, "No, Orso. You shall not kill him."

Orso was feeling weak and confused. He shook his head to clear his vision. It wasn't possible, but the l'il mousey seemed to be growing in front of his eyes. The l'il mousey was now big and strong … and was his chief.

Suddenly weary, the great bear sat down on his haunches. "Aw mousey," he groaned, disappointed … and then he fainted.

. . .

"Orso!" the little mouse cried. Then, to the man, who had seen life gripped back, literally, from the jaws of death, and had taken up his spear again, he commanded, "PUT THAT DOWN!"

The man stared, slack-jawed, unaware of the thud as his spear fell to the ground.

"Orso spared *your* life," the little mouse sternly directed, "now you will spare *his*."

The strength in the man's legs gave out abruptly. There was another jarring thud when he sat down. He bit his tongue hard enough to draw blood, but that, too, he did not notice.

"But … you're a *mouse*," he said, and then *he* fainted as well.

. . .

Orso's panting was shallow and rapid as his breath gusted across Kit's face. His jaws were slack, his tongue lolled in the dirt. Half-shut eyes were glassy harbingers of what must surely come.

Panic wanted to seize the mouse - to fill his mind, and force its will on him. So distraught was Kit, that there was a part of him that wanted to let the panic succeed – to just give up and run away - but he knew that was a luxury he couldn't afford, not while Orso lay dying. Instead, praying that the magic hadn't left him, he lay beside the mountain that was his friend, and forced himself to concentrate.

Amos, having sensed that the danger had passed, had uncurled himself, and now huddled quiet, but concerned. Soon he was joined by Lulu. She too, seemed to sense the need for quiet. She huddled as close as possible to the porcupine, almost as though she was seeking comfort from him. Then came Bumper, softly padding over from where he'd lain hidden until the danger was past. Now he crouched with the others, his nose twitching while he smelled Orso's life slipping away.

The little mouse was still … very still. He concentrated with all his might, but nothing was happening. He thought of the stars shining in the daylight sky. He thought of the wizened old mouse with the gentle voice, but still there was nothing.

It was he who had brought Orso to this place, and he thought that the bear's death would be a burden too heavy to endure. The spear had gone deep – he had seen the blow struck – had watched, horrified, as the shaft had sunk into his friend's body, and had seen the blood …

The blood …

Caught in mid-sentence, the transformation began.

The blood as it coursed through his body, gifting life – coursing … surging … weaker now … dwindling … but, still Life. As though his mind had become separated from his physical self, that part of him arose, and followed the passage of the wound deep into the bear's body. At length, he came to the great heart, and a sound like a leaking bellows. There was a cut, a very little cut, in the wall of the artery.

It was then that the voice of the wizened old mouse appeared in his mind.

Healing ... healing ... yessss ... yessss ...

Visions of his mother, his brothers and sisters all laughing and playing in the meadow.

Yesss ... healing ... healing ...

Visions of them curled up in their home at night ... hearing their reassuring heart-beats ... everyone safe ... everyone dreaming ...

There was so little blood left ... so little time.

Fire poured from his mind, searing the wound in the artery. Other, lesser veins had also been cut, these too he cauterized as his mind retreated out of the wound. Knitting and healing. Breath of wind ... and healing. Water – much water - to blood ... to healing.

When Kit blinked his little apple seed eyes, he was surprised to find that he was standing in sunshine.

Then, exhausted, he fainted, as well.

.   .   .

It was Chaser who revived him.

In his dream, he was back in the nest with his family, feeling warm and safe, when he felt the fawn's breath blowing softly over him. He didn't want to leave that happy place, but the breath was insistent. The effort seemed enormous, but he finally managed to open one reluctant eye.

Chaser smiled.

Over the fawn's shoulder, Rowena watched, concerned.

With further effort, Kit was able to rouse himself enough to notice the world around him. He must have been unconscious for a few minutes only, because both man and bear where still insensible. His head ached abominably.

Wincing from the pain, he noticed that Gort and Tod had re-joined the band (the fox limping painfully,) as well as the deer, and had settled in beside the others.

It was while he was wondering what might be done about his aching little head that the door to the cottage flew open, revealing a matronly woman, wild-eyed with fear, and a young man-child beside her. Both came running to where husband and father lay in the carrot patch, apparently without life.

The little mouse and the others nervously retreated to allow the woman and her son to come to the man. Without words being spoken, they stood protectively between the humans and Orso.

"Oh, Will!" cried the lady, "Are ye no more?" She was clearly distraught, her ashen face running freely with tears. She swooped down upon the man, cradling his head on her lap. The man-child, also ashen-faced, but determined, stooped down to pick up his father's spear.

Rowena came forward, and put a hoof upon the shaft. The boy frowned, and tried to wrest it away. The others crowded closer. Amos rattled his quills, both Gort and Tod growled deep in their chests, but it was when Lulu raised her tail that he reluctantly released his claim to the weapon.

The woman was weeping copious tears, raining them down upon her man's face. Then, in a matter of a second, her grief turned into shocked disbelief, and then joy, when his eyes fluttered open. For a moment, he didn't seem to recognise his wife, or realise where he was. Then, suddenly, he sat bolt upright, ignoring the woman's cries of astonishment and joy, and stared at the unconscious bear only a few feet away. Then, fearful, his head swivelled slowly around until he found Kit.

He stared, and stared.

"Please," said the little mouse, wincing, "may I have some water? I have a frightful headache."

The wife – saucer-eyed, now – shrieked, and shrieked, causing Kit to wonder that his head did not explode.

Then it was her turn to swoon.

.   .   .

Both son and man continued to stare with such open-mouthed amazement that the little mouse had to repeat himself several times before there was any other reaction.

At length, Will blinked his wonder down, but without taking his eyes away from Kit, he said to his son, "Go to the well, Walter, and fetch some water."

The boy stood as though he had sprouted roots, so the man repeated the command, only much louder. Galvanized to action, Walter leapt as though stung, and raced off to do as he was bidden.

After a while, still not taking his eyes off the little mouse, the man ventured, "Ye speak the High Tongue?"

"I speak to you, Will," the man's name felt foreign to Kit. "If that is your language, then yes, I speak the High Tongue." He turned to his companions, the thrill of magic still coursing through him, "And so do we all."

The man looked at the doe, the fawn, the hare, skunk, porcupine, fox and badger. All returned his stare, although all remained silent.

Will, unable to think of anything to say (because there was too much to say) also fell silent, and began to pluck painfully at the quills embedded in his legs.

"Here, let me help you," Kit offered, and concentrated on the barbed tips caught in the soft flesh of the man's leg. Slowly at first, but then more quickly as the Power took hold, the barbs metamorphosed into smooth, shiny needles that could be plucked with ease.

Once more, the man stared his amazement, first at the mouse, and then at the quills scattered on the ground at his feet.

Now Kit visualized water, and cool, soothing mud plastered to the angry wounds, a balm of healing into the tortured flesh.

Will felt the magic coursing over his legs, and stared at them as if they weren't his own. Without looking up, his voice shook with incredulity when he asked, "Ye are doing this, mouse?"

"Not I," Kit replied, "the Great Mouse is doing it through me."

"The Great Mouse?" The man pried his amazed eyes from his legs. Before he could question Kit further, he was overcome by the soothing of the magic. He sighed and reclined onto the garden's soft, tilled soil. If he must accept the existence of a magical talking mouse, a Great Mouse was of little matter.

Walter came running back with a pail and dipper. Vibrating with excitement, he offered some water to the little mouse. It was cold and sweet. Kit drank deeply, and felt much better.

"Thank you, Wal-ter," he said, this strange name also feeling foreign on his tongue. By way of a reply, the boy's excited grin threatened to separate the top of his head from the bottom.

However, when the little mouse bade him sprinkle some water onto the bear's tongue, the grin vanished, to be replaced with uncertainty.

Walter tore his eyes from the mouse to his father. Will considered, then shrugged, "Go ahead … but be careful."

The cold sweetness of the water on his tongue caused the bear to lap absently for more; but a tired smile, and a dreamy "Yum!" were as close as he came to waking.

Struck by an idea, the boy scooped a depression by the bear's snout. After lining it with a large cabbage leaf, he filled it with water from the bucket.

Orso's nose twitched as he picked up the scent. His smile widened a little, but he made no further effort to drink.

It was only after administering to the bear that either boy or man thought of the woman, lying unconscious on the ground.

Will started guiltily, "Walter, give us the dipper." He soaked a corner of his wife's dress, to sponge her face. When her eyes fluttered open, he held the dipper to her lips.

"Are ye all right, Nell?"

She took a short sip before pushing it aside, and – aided by her anxious husband - struggled upright.

She pointed shakily, "Th-th-the little mouse," she stammered, "it *spoke!*"

"Actually," Tod said, "he's *not* a little mouse, he's a very large, *friendly* mouse."

"I'b vewy happy!" quoth Gort, in a reflexive relapse.

"We're all friends," the deer chimed.

"I'm not bashful," Amos ventured.

Lulu fluttered her eyelashes shyly. "I smell pretty when I'm not frightened."

Bumper spoke last, but without much conviction. "Perhaps it isn't dangerous here?" he tailed off, rising to a doubtful interrogative.

This was too much for Nell. She had long since fluttered her eyes heavenward, before slumping back onto her husband's lap, once more unconscious.

A talking *mouse*, apparently, was all her mind was prepared to handle in one day.

.   .   .

"So the fire destroyed our homes," Kit said.

"It destroyed the grass," Rowena added.

"There wasn't any food," Bumper's ears drooped sadly.

"There wasn't much of anything," Gort grumbled crossly.

The companions, together with the humans, were grouped around the still unconscious Orso. Night had fallen, but when Will had suggested a fire, the animals had balked. That was when the story of the Great Fire came to light.

When the last words were spoken, Nell, now recovered, piped a tear from her eye.

"Ye poor lambs," she said. Then, with firm resolution, she said, "Ye'll not want while you're guests of this house."

Her husband shifted uncomfortably, but his

good wife rounded on him. Words were not spoken, but a powerful battle of wills was fought.

Finally admitting defeat, Will agreed.

"Ye saved my life, mouse," he allowed, "and as it happens, that's worth much to me and mine."

Both wife and son vigorously agreed.

"For such a deed," he continued solemnly, "let it not be said that Will Brown – known in these parts as Farmer Brown – lacked in his hospitality."

"Now then," Nell brightened, "that's been settled, Walter, there's two fat hens lying in the yard that need plucking, and I've a fine ham in the larder." She rose, carrying her corpulent body to her feet with surprising agility. Dusting the dirt from her dress, she said, "Best get started, we've hungry mouths to feed." Then, proudly to the companions, "I'll wager you've not tasted food the like as what you'll find at Nell Brown's table." Nodding primly, she and her son were about to return to the cottage, when there came a sound.

"Roots and honey?"

The words came in a deep, sleepy rumble.

Moonlight glittered off of one of the bear's tired eyes. Not quite awake, he offered Nell a groggy smile.

The good wife hesitated, and Will paled. This was a challenge that neither of them had foreseen, but before too many indecisive seconds had flown by, Nell nodded grimly.

"Aye, there's the honey pot newly filled this morning. Let me see, there's preserves of last year's blue berries, some apple butter ..." then wryly, "and I believe you've already acquainted yourself with our turnips." Then, in a low, sing-song voice, as though reciting an often spoken litany, she added, "Take all ye want, but eat all ye take. There's starving folk in far-off lands, and I'll not stand for waste."

Orso yawned, long and luxuriously.

"Okie-dokie, then."

He didn't understand much of what the nice lady said, but already he knew that it was best not to get on the wrong side of the cook.

.　.　.

"It was the king's men that burnt your forest," Will said, picking his teeth with a twig.

Everyone had been fed to bursting, even Orso. The admonition not to waste food was a serious one, and there was not a crumb, bone, leaf, nor dollop left to clutter the pile of empty platters that Mrs. Brown and her son carried back to the cottage. When they returned, she brought her husband's cloak, and a blanket for Walter and herself to keep out the night's chill.

Now with the licking of chops and grooming completed, the company settled down for more conversation. Filled stomachs beckoned sleep, but Will's words soon dispelled any chance of that.

"The King?" asked Kit, wide of eye.

"Burnt our forest?" queried a perplexed Tod.

"But, why?" groused Gort.

"We heard it from a wife down the way," Nell gestured vaguely with a tilt of her head. "*She* heard it from her son. *He* heard it from his best friend. *He* heard it from his lass that serves as a scullion maid in the castle." She leaned back, placing a hand on either ample knee. The triumphant look in her eye told all present that anything coming from her neighbour's son's best friend's lass could be naught but gospel true.

"They say it was a spark from a careless laid fire," the good wife continued in a storyteller's voice, designed to invoke awe. She needn't have bothered, for not a word was lost on the companions. "The summer had been dry, and the wind had been high," she continued dramatically, "The flames lit up the sky!"

"The king's men had made camp by the edge of the forest, and a spark must have jumped from their fire," Will said, arching an exasperated eyebrow at his wife. "The spark caught on the dry grass, and before anyone knew what was about, it had spread too fast to stop."

"Ohhhhh," the enlightened companions chorused.

"We don't go into the forest," said Will.

"They say it's enchanted," Walter explained.

"It is," said the little mouse.

"Aye," Will agreed with a rueful smile, "How else could I be talkin' to a mouse?"

"They say nowt but evil will come of it," the lady of the house whispered hoarsely with a fine, superstitious relish.

"Well, evil has certainly befallen *us*," Gort scowled.

Every one present had to agree that this much was true.

Reaching a decision, Kit said, "Tomorrow we will go to the castle, where your king can make amends."

Slow-spoken Will thought for a moment before venturing a reply. "That may, or may not be true," he said, doubtfully. "He's a good king, our Harry, but he may not see your lot the same as us."

"Aye," Nell agreed darkly, "he's a great lover of the hunt, that one."

Firmly, Will said, "When you can speak with a critter – when you sit down at table, and *eat* with 'em – well, it's different, ain't it?"

"T'would be murder," Nell agreed.

Now Will came to a decision. "When ye go tomorrow, be he King, and I only a lowly commoner, ye can count on Will Brown to be by your side. Mayhap I can be of some service."

The forest creatures started to thank him, but

he cut them short with a raised palm, and a gruff scowl, twinning himself with Gort.

"There's still the debt of my life that needs payin'," he explained. "And never let it be said that Will Brown doesn't repay what he owes."

"Perhaps that's true," replied the little mouse, "or perhaps you are nicer than you care to admit. Still, you and your family have all our thanks for everything that you've done for us."

Will tried another dark scowl, but looked pleased all the same. Walter blushed and grinned. Nell simpered horribly.

Then, with a grouchy reminder from Gort that the morning would arrive all too soon, the humans bade their guests a good night before retiring to their cottage.

Chained to the farthest corner of the yard, far enough away not to offend anyone's nose, Brutus howled pitifully when he saw them go.

The companions huddled around their giant friend, and, except for the little mouse, were soon fast asleep.

Lying awake under the night sky, Kit listened to their breathing in the still air. Orso's ribs shook and rumbled contentedly while someone murmured, restless in their sleep. Tomorrow would bring whatever it would bring, but at that moment, he couldn't remember ever feeling quite so safe, or quite so at home.

. . .

The Great Castle – which sat upon Castle Hill, and looked down upon the softly undulating lands of Castle Meadow – was the capital of the Great Kingdom, and so, the dwelling place of the king and his court.

A hard packed, gravelled road snaked up the steep incline of Castle Hill to the portcullis gates of the Great Castle, itself. Clattering up this road, late the next morning, followed by a train of his lords and huntsmen, came the king.

For Nell was right: hunting was the thing for Harold. He gloried in it. It gave him a zest for life. He was a good king, and popular with his subjects. He often said that hunting was a good excuse to go riding out on the fields on Lancer, his charger, and wave and talk to the people who would bow, and wave back wherever he went.

This morning, true to form, he had arisen early, and summoning his favourite lords and finest huntsmen, had ridden forth to try their luck with their hawks, hounds, bows, and boar spears.

It had been necessary for it to be a short outing, for today was not just any other day. Today, in fact, was the day that Princess Mary, his beautiful daughter, would choose a man from her myriad of suitors to be her husband.

The king had thought to stay out longer, but a strict and severe lecture from the queen had killed any such notion in its infancy.

"This is your daughter's special day." She had shaken a stern finger to impress the point upon him.

When she shook her finger like that, he knew that it was in his best interest to pay attention.

"You are her father, and the king. We must both," she had frowned, and then repeated, "*both* be in attendance when she decides."

Harold thought that this was poor fare when compared to the thrill of chasing a fox over hill and through dale, but he knew better than to argue.

"Yes, my dear," he murmured unhappily, but left immediately before his wife forbade him from any hunting that day, at *all*.

It hadn't been a very successful morning's work – just a brace of hares for the pot - but as Harold put Lancer to the steep slope of Castle Road on Castle Hill, he was surprised when he discovered that he didn't mind very much.

This was, after all, Mary's day, and as the morning had progressed, he found that he was becoming untypically sentimental about it.

Mary – dear, sweet Mary! It seemed as though it was only yesterday that she had been born, and then the screaming little bundle had reminded him more of a little mouse than a princess. In fact, all through her days, that had been his own, private name for her – their own little secret – Little Mouse.

The king heaved a heavy sigh. He supposed that his daughter would no longer be his little mouse after she became a respectable wife. That thought made him sad.

Lancer's hooves clattered across the cobbled courtyard as the train entered the castle. Harold tossed the reins to a page before dismounting, then gave the stallion an affectionate slap on the neck, before hurrying to the palace, to prepare for the ceremony.

The guards at the gate clanged to attention as he approached.

"Well, Tom," he affably addressed the one on

the right. He knew his men called him 'Good ol' Harry' behind his back, and it pleased him. "How's that little imp of yours?"

The new father grinned proudly. "Growin' more and more every day, Your Highness."

"Treasure her, Tom. Treasure her." The king clapped him on the shoulder, one father to another.

"That I will, Your Highness."

"And you, Ned," Harold turned to the guard on the left, "I hear your good lady is expecting again."

Ned dourly nodded his assent. "That is true, Your Highness."

"How many will that make? Five … six?"

"Seven, Your Highness."

"Seven? Bless me, but you've been hard at it, haven't you?"

"It helps pass the nights, sire," Ned allowed.

"Well, you're a good man, Ned."

The guardsman considered this gravely. "Should Your Highness ever have the opportunity of mentioning that fact within hearing of my missus, I would be most obliged. Lately, she seems to be entertaining quite a different opinion."

Harold laughed. "It's like that, is it? Well, ne'er mind, she'll see differently once she comes to term."

Ned looked him squarely in the eye. "One *fervently* hopes so, sire."

.  .  .

The gates of the palace opened onto the Great Hall, and it was this hall – down which Harold now tramped on his way to the Great Staircase – that was lined with his hunting trophies.

To the left, a stag's head was fastened to the wall, a great, spider's web of antlers, at least six feet across, cast shadows on the tiled floor.

He remembered that kill as though it were only yesterday. He and that buck had been sparring for years, but he'd got him in the end. One arrow, straight through the heart. Damned good shot it was, too.

On the right was the ugly, tusked head of a boar.

That scarred old veteran had been a legend in the kingdom for years, but he'd winkled him out eventually. It had been a bit of a lucky thrust, really. The scoundrel had been chased out of the brush, practically under Lancer's feet.

Further along, past elk, panther, bison, and antelope, he came to his pride and joy.

A giant bear, stood rampant, towering a good ten feet if he was an inch. His jaws had been wired open in an eternal roar, revealing fangs as long as daggers. Forelegs spread wide, showed to the best effect, the great scythe-like claws.

Hurried as he was, Harold took the time to pause by the savage old monster. It was his way of doing it honour.

"That was quite the battle we had, wasn't it, old warrior?" He smiled, wistful with the memory. "We shan't see your like any time soon." Then, with no more time to spare, he was racing up the Great Stairway to his chambers, shouting for his valet. "Smithers! Blast, where is the fellow? Oh, there you are."

As usual, Smithers, waiting patiently, opened the door just as the king arrived.

"Will Your Highness care to bathe?" he asked with an elegant bow. "The water has been drawn."

"No," Harold hated baths, "no time today, Smithers."

The valet twitched one eyebrow the merest fraction of an inch. "Her majesty Juliana expressly instructed …"

"Oh, very well!" the king cried irritably, holding his arms out to be disrobed. After twenty years of marriage, he had learned to pick his battles, and to pick one today, he knew, would not be wise.

Two minutes later, he was gingerly easing himself into the steaming tub, whereupon Smithers, with an air of immense importance, sprinkled decanters of scented oils and bathing salts into the water, as befitted a king.

Harold held out a resigned arm, and the valet promptly set about it with a bar of perfumed soap, a scrub brush, and cloth.

Smithers knew that the king hated to bathe, he had ever since he was a lad; so he knew that conversation would be needed to lighten the dudgeon hanging over the room, and there was only one conversation that would fit the bill.

"Was Your Highness served with good fortune this morning?"

The king scowled, "Brace of hares, nothing more."

"Perhaps Your Highness will have greater luck on the morrow."

Harold's scowl deepened. "Not much chance of that, I'm afraid. There hasn't been good hunting around these parts in donkeys' years. I expect that it's all been hunted out."

It was true; there had been a dirth of game for the past few years. Every morning the king set forth with great expectations, only to return in the evening with very little but frustration to show for his pains.

"Poachers, d'you think, sire?"

"No one would dare!" The king splashed angrily at the very idea. "I'd have them drawn and quartered!"

The truth of the matter was that Harold had been having such a splendid time, slaughtering everything in sight, that his head gamekeeper had been afraid to inform him that he was solely responsible for driving the kingdom's wildlife to the brink of extinction. It was well recognised among the household staff that, in order to maintain any equanimity at court, that knowledge should remain a secret from their master.

Then Smithers brightened … which is to say, he almost smiled.

"There have been," he said, "reports of a bear, sire."

The king frothed around in the tub so suddenly that it very nearly upset.

"A bear?"

"Yes, sire."

"Where away?"

"The common folk say from lands abutting the Enchanted Forest, Your Highness."

"The Enchanted Forest?" The king's brow furrowed. "That's strange, wouldn't you say, Smithers?"

"I would, indeed, Your Highness."

The king's frown deepened, and a pall seemed to descend over the room. Talk of the Enchanted Forest had reminded him of the Great Fire. His men had claimed that it had been an accident, but they were such superstitious fools, one never knew. It was possible that it had been set on purpose. The forest was said to be possessed by demons, and folklore had it that such things could only be destroyed in flames.

Harold sighed. Accident or design, in the end it made little difference.

"A bad business, Smithers," he mused ruefully, "a bad business all around."

"It is, indeed, sire."

Smithers knew, as did all in the household, that the destruction of the Enchanted Forest greatly troubled the king. Superstition notwithstanding, everyone knew that it was best to leave the place alone. Whenever it had been trifled with in the past, there had always been a reckoning.

Wishing to dispel the gloom, Smithers thought to change the subject. If the king's first love wasn't the ticket, then his second love would have to do.

"Forgive my impertinence, sire," Smithers smirked, now taking cloth and scrub brush vigorously to the royal back, "but has Your

Highness pondered, at all, upon the choice that the Princess Mary might make?"

The crease on Harold's brow smoothed. He chuckled affectionately.

"Could be any one of the young rascals," he laughed indulgently. "All good family. All good boys. Some hunt better than others," he allowed, "but they'll learn, eh? *I* did."

.   .   .

The Princess Mary paced nervously, back and forth, from the window to the door in deep agitation. Today was her eighteenth birthday, the day she must choose her consort, and she had to admit that she just wasn't sure.

"I suppose that I love Johnny," she said irritably. "He's quite handsome and attentive, and everything. But, Mother, he can be such a child at times!"

Her mother, the Queen, was seated on the Princess' bed, watching her daughter pacing back and forth with all the appearance of calm that she could muster. She felt that *someone* should appear to be calm, but all the same, she was feeling a growing frustration with her daughter.

"Well, dear," she began, "men *are* such children, at times, aren't they? I mean, you have only to look at your father to see that, don't you? I happen to think that Prince John is an excellent choice, by the way."

"Yes, but," the Princess made a slight, dismissive gesture, "Daddy's so … so …"

"Biddable?" her mother suggested.

The Princess darted her mother a look that somehow managed to be both annoyed and guilty.

Juliana laughed.

"Oh, Darling," she smiled, "you can't imagine that he was that way when I married him? No," she shook her head, soberly, "marriage takes work. I have long seen that, if I am to be any part of your father's life at all, I would have to be quite firm with him. I mean, he's always away, isn't he? I'm sensible enough to know that he must feel that he has *some* freedom, but I always rein him in before he gets too many ideas."

"Oh, Mother!" the Princess paused, mid-stride, "That sounds perfectly dreadful."

"Does it?" the Queen asked with a wistfulness masked by unconcern, "I suppose that it might to someone so young."

"Well," Mary resumed her pacing, "I don't want my husband to be *biddable*," she pronounced the word with dry distaste. "I want him to be ... oh, I don't know! I want him to be the other half of who I am, I suppose."

"Whatever that means," her mother replied with slight agitation. Then she rose from the bed and took her daughter's hands in her own, giving them a slight shake periodically to give emphasis to her words.

"Dear Mary," she said, "you are eighteen today, old enough to be a queen in your own right – old enough to rule. These romantic notions of yours are all fine and well, for a commoner, I suppose, but a *queen*," she paused, emphasizing heavily, "cannot afford to be ruled by her heart."

For a moment, the princess' eyes flared in rebellion. She was, after all, her mother's daughter, and a fiery temper was part of it; but she was also her father's daughter – her dear, sweet, *biddable* father – and that was part of it, too.

"Of course, Mother," she lowered her eyes, and willed the fire from them. "You are right ... as always."

Juliana patted her daughter's hand, "There, there, child, you're just having a case of nerves, that's all, which is only natural. Why, when I was your age, I was near out of my mind with anxiety."

Suddenly the princess asked, "Do you have regrets, Mother?"

"Regrets?" Her mother's surprise caused her to enunciate perhaps a shade too sharply. She drew herself erect, her head regal and proud. "I am Queen!"

Perhaps she felt that that was answer enough, but although she decided not to push the subject any further, Mary did not.

"Come now, my dear," the Queen chided irritably, "enough of this foolishness. Prince John will make a perfect match. He will rule the lands to the west of the Great Kingdom one day, and you shall rule with him. Then, in time, you shall have this kingdom as well. Now really, does that sound so bad?"

Mary shrugged, but said nothing.

Recognising the gesture, the queen felt her irritation return, but the moment was saved by a subtle knock on the door.

"Come!" Juliana called.

The door opened, and the Princess' maidservant entered. Bobbing a curtsy, she said, "Beg pardon, ma'am, but my lady's dress is here. It's time for her to prepare for the Ball."

"Then I shall leave you to it," the Queen replied with a sense of relief. She turned to the Princess, "I shall see you downstairs, daughter." Then, reacting to Mary's woebegone appearance, she placed a hand on her arm, "Try not to look so glum, dear, it shall come right, in the end." Then, having exhausted her supply of maternal advice, she left without another word.

.   .   .

The companions were making their way down Castle Road. There was a sense of urgency: Orso was hungry.

Well, they were all hungry, weren't they?

Farmer Brown's wife had fed them breakfast, but they had been traveling hard, and the sun was hot. Although Nell had given Will several sacks of food for Godwin, their mule, to carry, most of that had already been consumed. For all of the little mouse's healing, the great bear was weak, and badly in need of nourishment. For the time being, Kit had cast the spell of an illusory fullness, but he wasn't sure how long that would last.

Amos, Lulu, and Gort were trying their best, but they were footsore, unused to such a gruelling pace. For the rest, Rowena, Chaser, and Bumper were doing well enough, even Tod was keeping up. Yesterday's eve, the little mouse had ministered to his leg. No bone had been broken, but the bruise had been deep. Much concentrating on cool water, wind, and healing earth had been needed to reduce the swelling, and as a result, Kit, himself, was tired. He had tried to keep up, but he was just a little mouse, and his legs would not answer to the pace that was demanded. Before they had gone too far, Will, having seen his predicament, had scooped him up, and placed him on Godwin's back.

At first Kit had been terrified to be perched at such a dizzy height above the ground, and he had clung onto the mule's coat, trying not to cry out in fear; but after the miles had drifted by beneath him, he rather came to enjoy the experience. In the end, after asking politely for permission, he had crawled up Godwin's neck, until he sat, perched between his ears.

It was such a thrill, riding so high; he felt that he could see to the end of the earth, and remarked as much to the mule.

Godwin – a rather morose fellow – replied that he would get used to it, soon enough.

The little mouse had spoken with Will that morning before they had set out. He hadn't any fixed plan in his mind, or any plan at all outside of confronting the king, and demanding retribution.

"In that case," Will had said, scratching the back of his head, "confront him we shall, my small friend, and face to face at that." So they had chosen to take Castle Road, not bothering with concealment.

Castle Road was the kingdom's main highway, and the traffic had been unusually heavy – heavier than even Will had ever seen. There were the usual carts, and wagons carrying produce and wares to market, but in addition, there had been more than a few trains of great lords and ladies. Some were on horseback, some in carriages, even some travelled in covered sedan chairs slung between two mules. All were making their way towards the Great Castle.

Will had been worried about the 'critters' – as he called them – encountering humans along the way, especially that great beast of a bear, and they had drawn more than a few curious stares, and once or twice, horses had panicked when Orso's scent wafted into their nostrils. Then the rider had to hang on for dear life while his steed bucked and pitched, until either they were safely past, or the man was flung onto the road.

More than a few had threatened to take action, but Will had boldly declared that this was the king's highway, and that all might travel freely. This was greeted with dark looks and much grumbling, for Will was just a lowly peasant, and they were from the most noble families in the land; but all thought better than to interfere, with the bear standing so threateningly close beside him.

For his part, Orso wasn't comfortable with all of this unsought attention, but Mousey had said that they must go to the stony castle right quick-quick, and Mousey was his chief. For the bear – who didn't like to clutter his mind with too many details – that was enough.

Be that as it may, there was no getting away from the fact that Orso was hungry, and tired. Roots and Honey, he felt that he had never *been* so tired! His massive feet plodded along the gravel surface, scuffing up dust that got in his nose, making him sneeze. He felt light headed, and wanted to lie down to rest, but Mousey said they couldn't stop. Mousey had never said why they couldn't stop - perhaps he didn't know himself - but he had been insistent.

That much was true: Kit felt an urgency to reach the Great Castle. He didn't know why, but it had to be tonight – tomorrow wouldn't do. If they didn't soon reach their destination, he felt that they all might be in great danger.

As the afternoon stretched into the evening, he measured the distance to the castle looming ahead of them, and then tried to gauge the strength left in his weary companions.

He fretted, and begged them for more speed.

Then he fretted some more.

.   .   .

The position of King's Valet had been a Smithers' family tradition since time immemorial. His father had faithfully served Harold's father, then his grandfather the royal grandfather before that, for as long as the kingdom had existed. This was not terribly uncommon of the household of the Great Castle. Several families could boast centuries of faithful service to their royalty, but none longer than Smithers', nor none so close to those in power.

It was Harold's great grandsire, Hengist, who had decreed that, in recognition of his family's loyal service, the scions of the house of Smithers would, from that time on, be rewarded with the post of major domo, as well as personal valet to His Majesty, and so it had transpired.

Although he would have died before ever dreaming of admitting as much, Smithers loved his station as major domo. He rather fancied that the prestigious post suited his own sense of importance, and he especially loved his official staff of office.

On special occasions, such as this night, for instance, he would take his position at the entrance to the ballroom, and as guests arrived, he would gravely bash the silver-girded heel of the staff three times onto the stone flags of the floor, before bellowing each guest's name and titles to all of the great ones assembled. Only someone of immense importance, and impeccable bearing, could be given such a position, and Smithers was determined that no one in the kingdom should carry their person quite so importantly, or so impeccably, as he did himself.

Now, as the orchestra played soft music in the balcony, and the king and queen sat with regal composure upon their thrones, Smithers felt a surge of pure pleasure thrill through to his bones.

He, as well as the rest of the household, was dressed in his best livery, except that, of course, as major domo, his was better, and quite different, from everyone else. His robes were of the finest scarlet silk, his shoes of the softest calfskin. Gauntleted, kidskin gloves, and a brilliant yellow velvet cap - complete with ostrich feather, fastened with a diamond pin - completed the magnificence of his finery; and of course, in his gloved right hand, was grasped his silver-bound staff of office.

There was a stirring outside in the Great Hall, and Smithers drew himself to attention.

The guests were arriving; soon it would be Show Time.

·　·　·

The sun had been set for an hour by the time that the companions arrived at the base of Castle Hill.

By now, there was no more traffic on Castle Road. The market had closed for the day, and all of the lords and ladies had long since passed them by.

All wanted to rest before ascending the steep path, but the little mouse was very fretful. Time was short, and there was not a moment to lose.

So, amidst pitiful complaints of aching feet, and stiff limbs, not to mention empty bellies, Will, leading Godwin by his halter, led the way up Castle Hill, with the others following in various states of exhaustion.

.   .   .

"Sir R-r-r-oger R-r-r-edvers of R-r-r-otha!" Smithers bellowed proudly, thoroughly enjoying rolling his R's.

A tall, thin young man, dressed from head to toe in velvet of emerald green, entered the ballroom, and made his way to the dais.

At the base of the platform, two chairs (both elaborately carved, covered with gold leaf, and crimson cushions) sat, side by side.

The Princess Mary, pale but beautiful, in heavy silk brocade, sat unhappily upon the chair to the left. The one to the right was empty.

At a respectful thirty paces from the dais, the

young man swept into an elegant bow.

The king and queen gravely inclined their royal heads to Sir Roger. The Princess Mary jerked her own head so nervously, that she very nearly dislodged her gold, and jewelled crown.

Sir Roger paused, expectantly.

Mary sat, still as a statue.

Juliana cleared her throat just loudly enough for the Princess to hear.

Stung to action, Mary gestured feebly at the chair by her side, "Please sir, do be seated."

The young gallant approached and bowed once more, this time accepting the hand she offered, then pecked its knuckles perfunctorily, before settling into the chair.

This was the time-honoured tradition of the land. On the night of a princess' eighteenth birthday, suitors would take the seat that Sir Roger now occupied, and converse with the object of their devotion. There, while everyone pretended not to notice, the young man would press his suit. This could take the form of anything: from declaring his love, engaging to be entertaining, and/or amusing, or even to something that more closely resembled a business proposition. All would be designed to win either the girl's heart or mind, and thereby gain her hand in holy – and stately - matrimony.

The time spent thus varied drastically, as it depended entirely upon how the princess responded to her suitor. Should he please her, then he would be allowed to remain; but should the King and Queen sense that their daughter was not happy with her present company, a discreet signal would be given, and the young man – along with his dreams of a blissful union with the Princess – would be whisked away to pine elsewhere.

Sir Roger spent the next five minutes speaking long and volubly about himself, his land, his hounds, and his money.

The Princess Mary sat stiff, back straight as a pole, not joining in the conversation. Eventually, she darted appealing looks over her shoulder to her father.

At length, the king rubbed the side of his nose with a surreptitious forefinger, and a courtier approached the young man, swept into the courtliest of bows, and begged him to 'pray do partake of the banquet' that several, groaning tables were endeavouring to support along one wall of the ballroom.

Aghast, Sir Roger stopped mid-sentence. Plainly, he had expected that he, and his land, hounds, and money had been an unbeatable combination to the Princess Mary's heart, and, he had hoped, her avarice. Faced with the fact that this was not to be the case, he seemed at a loss as to what to do next.

However, when the courtier repeated his invitation, this time with the slightest edge to his voice, he saw that there was nothing to be done. After all, he reasoned, if the silly girl didn't know what she was about, it was no fault of his.

Attempting nonchalance, but blushing furiously, Sir Roger rose and managed an exit, while all the nobility of the land showed their breeding by affecting to look elsewhere.

No sooner was he gone than there came the thunderous Boom!...Boom!...Boom! as Smithers, brimming with self-importance, bashed the butt of his staff onto the floor.

"His R-r-r-r-oyal Highness Pr-r-r-r-ince

John of Agr-r-r-r-r-r-ravia! And his R-r-r-r-royal R-r-r-r-r-r-retinue!"

The room fell into a hush, as a fine well-muscled young man swept into the room, dressed in silks of royal blue and gold, with a golden circlet upon his handsome brow. With lordly steps, he made his way to the dais while his entourage filed silently to the side.

So beautiful and noble was this young man, so impressive was his bearing, that a smattering of spontaneous applause marked his progress down the length of the room. When he swept into his bow, a maiden in the crowd collapsed in a swoon.

Harold warmly smiled his welcome. His Queen smirked knowingly.

Mary offered the prince a shy smile, and indicated the chair next to her.

"Please My Lord, do be seated."

.   .   .

The companions were nearing the great gates. Guards, armed and armoured, stood to either side.

Perched between Godwin's ears, Kit felt his mouth go dry with fear. As if sensing this, Will, turned and muttered, "Whatever plan you've got up your sleeve, mouse, now would be the time to put it into action."

However, the little mouse had neither a plan, nor a sleeve to put it in, and hadn't even known that he would have need of one. Now seeing the burly guards in their shining armour, and their long, dangerous, sharp looking spears blocking the way, he wondered how he could ever have been so foolish.

Once more, Will half-turned, "Well?"

"Keep going."

Who had said that? Was it himself?

Will, too, was surprised. He had stiffened, and had begun to turn around.

"Keep going, I say! If you hesitate, all is lost!"

Will managed to check himself in time, continuing on with scarcely a break in stride. Such a voice, well schooled to command, could not be ignored.

That's when the kindly old voice spoke in Kit's mind.

"You must not be afraid, little mouse," it said, "all will yet be well."

It was then that he began to feel the Power

surging inside of him, once more.

Earth, Wind, Fire, and Water!

Huge torrents coursed out of him, surging vertically, before dividing at its apex, like water from a fountain, to cascade to earth forming a protective umbrella around himself and his companions. The deafening torrent roared in his ears, drowning out all other sounds.

The guards never moved. Neither did they appear to have witnessed anything unusual. Incredibly, they continued leaning on their spears as though they were the most bored people in the kingdom ... which, if the truth be told, they were.

Filled with wonder, the little mouse gazed all around, noticing that his companions, while tired, and perhaps grumbling under their breath from their arduous journey, still followed loyally behind, and none seemed to notice the powerful magic that was inundating them.

Then, as suddenly as it had started, the channel of Power abruptly stopped, hanging suspended over the company, for what seemed like an eternity. Then, with a crash and a roar, it fell, washing over them all, bathing each in magic.

"Now, behold your companions," the soft voice instructed, with perhaps just a tiniest hint of pride.

The first change he noticed was in Godwin. Instead of finding himself perched between the ears of a plodding mule, Kit discovered that he was now seated on a fine, silver-embossed saddle, upon an even finer snow-white stallion.

The next he noticed was himself.

In his hands (his *hands*?) he held soft reins. His long, hose-encased legs gripped either side of Godwin's flanks, and his feet, booted and silver-spurred, were inserted into argent stirrups.

He took one of his new hands, and filled with wonder, felt the texture of his new satin doublet, then timidly, the cloth cap perched upon his head.

Next there was Will. Gone was the simple, rough garb of the peasant. In its place were hose and doublet of fine material of forest green. Emblazoned on his chest was an oak tree, above which a disembodied eye seemed to fix him with its hypnotic stare.

Turning in his saddle, the little mouse saw that his companions had also assumed human form, and were similarly attired. The exception being that, whereas Will's dress was green, each of the forest creatures bore the colour and pattern of their original coat.

The giant with the vacant grin, dressed in tawny brown, could be none other than Orso. The beautiful, doe-eyed lady in the dun-coloured dress, Rowena, with her handsome, similarly clad, son walking at her side. Then came a dapper Tod in burnt orange, Gort, resplendent

(but still saturnine) in silver and black, Lulu, also in black, but with a wide stripe of white, Bumper in salt and pepper, and Amos in an extravagant charcoal of shimmering needles. Emblazoned on every breast was a crest bearing an oak tree, all with the same gleaming eye.

"They are unaware of their transformation," the kindly, old voice whispered, as if in his ear. "They see one another unchanged, as they have always been. Although others shall see them as you do."

As if in confirmation, the guards suddenly erased their bored expressions, and sprang to attention.

When the party arrived at the gate, Ned, with a curious glance at their coat of arms, asked, "Your pass, milord?"

And there it was, in Kit's hand, a roll of parchment bound with green ribbon. Striving mightily to disguise his astonishment, he offered it to the guardsman.

Ned accepted it with thanks, undid the ribbon, and unrolled the scroll. As he scanned down the page, his eyes widened, and even in the feeble torchlight, the little mouse could see that the colour had drained from his face.

Having finished, Ned darted a nervous glance at his companion before returning the scroll. All the while, he made no attempt to hide his astonishment.

"You may pass, Your Highness," he said. The whites of his eyes glowed unnaturally bright in the moonlit evening.

Hiding his confusion, Kit took the pass from Ned's nervously extended hand, and nudged Godwin with his knees. And that was all there was to it - they were through.

Will turned with blank amazement. "How did you manage that?"

"The Great Mouse is with us, Will. Tonight is a night for strong magic."

The simple farmer stared at the little mouse perched between his mule's ears. Inexplicably, for the first time, he was afraid.

"These are strange happenings beyond my ken," he said, taking up Godwin's halter with one hand, while crossing himself with the other, "and mayhap, I would keep it that way."

A liveried servant, bowing low, had met them inside the gate, and served as a guide to the palace. Whereupon, he murmured that he begged milord to enter, and that he, personally, would take milord's steed to the royal stables if milord should so wish it.

Kit swung down from the saddle, half-expecting a strange experience, to be standing on two feet, but he found this not to be the case. It felt as though he had been walking upright all his life.

Will hesitated, at a loss. His rustic sense of honour told him that he should go with the companions, but he found that strong magic daunting, and wished to be rid of it.

Seeing his friend's indecision, the little mouse said, "Go with him, Will. You've helped us far beyond what we had a right to expect." When the good farmer still hesitated, he added, "Go now, all will be well."

Will overcame his stubborn indecision, and surreptitiously making the sign against strong magic, said. "Aye, mayhap I've helped you all that I'm able. What else shall happen this night, I shall be a stranger to, as it will have surpassed my poor understanding."

Then, wishing all of them continued good fortune, he allowed himself to be led away by the curious, but politely silent servant, with Godwin in tow.

The human visitors held no monopoly on curiosity. All day, the companions had been meeting new and wondrous creatures, but now, within the bowels of the Great Castle, they unconsciously huddled together while they gazed about the stone ramparts, and buildings, even forgetting their hunger for the moment, in this alien world.

Now as Kit stepped across the threshold, into the palace, they (none of whom had set hoof or paw in a building before) still nervously huddled together like freshly-hatched chicks, and - counter to every instinct they possessed - followed.

.   .   .

A young page, bowing most correctly, met them at the door, and preceded them down the length of the Great Hall, past Harold's trophies along the wall.

Rowena was the first to scream. For there, mounted high up on the wall, his antlers casting wide shadows onto the stone flags of the floor, and gazing down upon them through eyes of glass, was the head of her father.

.　　.　　.

Within the ballroom, the shriek was quite audible, causing much consternation among all assembled.

Ignoring his wife's astonishment, Harold signed for the Sergeant at Arms to investigate. Then, rising to his feet, he announced to the room at large, "Please, My Lords, and Ladies, do not be alarmed. I'm sure that it is nothing to cause you concern. Pray, continue with the festivities!"

High up in the balcony, the musicians hesitated, as indeed, the entire room had frozen to silence. However, at an impatient gesture from the king, they resumed their playing, filling the room with soft music, gradually soothing distraught nerves. The scream had been such a dreadful sound.

Soon the ballroom returned to normal, although many could not restrain themselves from casting curious glances past Smithers to the Great Hall beyond.

.   .   .

"Rowena!" Kit knelt beside the doe who had fallen into a faint. Unable to think of what to do next, he took off his cap, and fanned her face.

The others, filled with concern, had crowded around.

"What happened?" Lulu asked.

It was Chaser, deathly pale, and trembling, who supplied the answer.

Indicating the head mounted on the wall, he said, "That was my grand-sire." Then he burst into tears.

"What's this? What's going on here?" Striding self-importantly, the Sergeant at Arms inserted himself into the little throng. When he beheld the beautiful lady, sallow of face, and unconscious upon the floor, he angrily demanded, "What's wrong with her?"

Unfortunately, as the others struggled for words to explain, at that moment, Orso spied the great stuffed bear at the foot of the stairway.

.   .   .

The first indication to the guests that, contrary to what the King had assured them, all was *not* well, was when the Sergeant at Arms came flying through the doorway to crash in an unconscious heap, amongst the tables and guests at the buffet.

The second was when a grim and angry giant of a man appeared through the door a heartbeat later. On his chest was emblazoned a curious design of an oak tree with something that looked like an eye poised above it.

Seeing their chief fall, the guards came rushing to his defence with drawn steel, past roaring lords, and screaming ladies. Blood would very likely have been shed, right there and then, but for a loud, commanding voice.

"ORSO, NO!"

The enraged giant, looking every bit as though he would like nothing better than to take on the entire palace guard, hesitated. Still not taking his eyes off of his adversaries, he called, as though remonstrating, "But Mousey!"

It was then that the owner of that commanding voice appeared at the doorway, and it was here that all assembled were given their first impression of him.

Tall, dark, and dressed head to toe in the richest finery, Kit stepped into the room, oblivious of anyone but Orso. Placing a hand on his arm, he said, "Not like this, my friend. You must leave it to me."

However, seeing his Sergeant at Arms apparently assaulted, Harold was now on his feet, livid with anger.

"Guards!" he shouted, "Arrest these people!"

Then, to the astonishment of everyone, including herself, Mary cried, "No, Father!"

Unaware that she had done so, she leapt from her chair (where she had been listening patiently while Prince John spoke in loving terms of his latest kite), and was running down the length of the room to place herself protectively between this stranger and her father's guardsmen.

The men-at-arms, finding their points now levelled at their Princess' breast, lowered their swords, uncertain as to what to do next.

"Daughter, come away from that dangerous fellow," her father commanded, striding down the length of the room. His own sword rasped from its scabbard as he came on.

"Put away your weapon, oh King!" That strong stentorian voice commanded, and the young man brushed aside a guardsman to confront Harold.

The guard, sensing that his king might be in danger, made to hold the young man back, but behind him, the glowering giant delivered a lightning blow to his head that, if not for his helmet, would almost certainly have crushed his skull. As it was, he joined his chief under the buffet, in the land of dreams.

"Orso!" the man cried, but aside from ensuring that his own chief remained unmolested, the giant made no further effort to intervene.

Seeing his daughter out of immediate danger, the king hesitated, then faced with those commanding coal-dark eyes, he lowered his point.

"Who are you, sir," he demanded, "and what mean you by this outrage?"

"As to outrage, sire," the young man retorted angrily, "I will demand as much of you, and what manner of creatures you be. As to who I am," he offered a small roll of parchment, neatly tied with green ribbon, "this will suffice to answer."

Harold gestured to Smithers who had been hovering nervously on the periphery. The major domo gingerly accepted the parchment from Kit's hand. Untying the ribbon, he held it out before him, unrolled it, and read.

Like Ned at the gate, he too, blanched. Then his eyes bulged.

"Well?" the King snapped impatiently, "Out with it, man!"

Smithers looked from the parchment to the young man, then to the crest on his chest. Finally, he looked to Harold. "Your Highness," he said, his voice badly shaken, "may I present the Prince of the Enchanted Forest."

He completely forgot to roll a single R.

At this, a great hubbub arose. It grew into an uproar when the rest of Kit's companions timidly entered the room. The cries of astonishment were because now they could see a hare, a porcupine, a fox, a badger, a skunk, and a very frightened, and distressed - but also very determined - doe with her fawn.

More than everything else, the shouting was for the great bear that loomed where the giant had been only a moment before.

A bear, Harold thought, so the rumours were true. Of all the companions, only Kit remained a human.

He felt someone clutch his arm. Looking down, he felt a jolt of lightning, stronger than any magic he had felt before, when he saw the lovely princess returning his stare. He had never seen anyone quite so beautiful.

As for the Princess Mary, she had been in love from the moment this stranger had entered the room. Something – call it intuition – said that this was not a biddable man, but someone with whom she could walk side by side through all the days of her life.

The uproar had become deafening. Harold held up a hand, commanding silence. When the tumult gradually died down, he returned his attention to the young man in green.

"What is the meaning of this sorcery?" He had tried to sound angry, but in his heart he knew, and the knowing robbed his voice of authority.

There could be no mistake. These wild creatures guarding their strange, young prince, and that crest of tree and eye, left all doubt behind. The burning of the Enchanted Forest had returned to haunt him.

"Are you our reckoning?" he asked, but it wasn't really a question.

Kit tore his eyes away from the beautiful creature on his arm.

"We come for recompense, King," he replied, his steely voice, as of yet, containing the full force of his anger.

Harold nodded ruefully.

"Ever since that terrible night," he said, "I have often wondered what the price might be."

His beloved daughter's gaze of naked adoration had not been lost on him. "But, this price is too high, sir." His tone gained strength. "Come man, ours is a wealthy kingdom, all the riches of which may be yours for the asking. I do freely admit that that unfortunate burning was of our doing." He drew himself up proudly. "Although it was no fault of mine, I am King, and must bear responsibility." Then, with steel of his own giving edge to his meaning, he added, "Have yon great brute take my life, if you will, but you shall not take my only child."

By way of a reply, Kit did not deign to answer with words. Instead, he glowered angry flames of Power into the eyes of the King.

Harold stood transfixed, his own fury impotent in the grip of the spell. He was aware of the room spinning around him, faster and faster until everything but those soul-piercing eyes were just a blur.

Shaken, he put a hand to his brow to steady himself. When he withdrew it, he found that he was no longer in the ballroom, or, indeed, in the palace. He was no longer even in the Great Castle, because he was no longer the king.

Instead he was Pendarch, the great stag.

.   .   .

They – he with his does and their fawns – were in a meadow where the grass was sweet, and a stream gurgled peacefully nearby. The sun was warm, luring him into a doze. A beautiful day, it felt good to be alive.

Suddenly, he raised his head, sensing danger. In the distance, carried on the wind, he could hear the hounds belling their thirst for blood.

They were drawing nearer.

He knew that there wasn't a moment to lose. The does and fawns had grouped together at the first sound of the dogs – all but little Rowena, who stood paralyzed with fear amongst the bluebells.

He bounded over to her, nudging her toward the others.

"Quickly, Little Mouse," he had always called her that, "to your dame!"

Spurred by the urgency, the fawn leapt

forward towards a doe who had been frantically calling to her.

He urged the herd across the stream. The hounds were too close now, he would have to lead them away from his family.

"Run!" he called to the lead doe, "Keep running until you reach the forest, they dare not follow. Remain there until I re-join you."

With that, he was bounding off in the other direction, determined to lead the dogs away.

From out of nowhere, he felt a sharp pain drive deep into his chest, then he saw the feathered shaft. He tried to run, but his legs refused to obey. He crashed to the earth, and struggled to rise, but already the hounds were on him, biting and rending, devouring him while he yet lived.

Then one of the dogs was whipped aside, and he looked up to see himself, King Harold, and he was *laughing*. The king took him by the antlers, forcing back his head, and he felt a slicing pain across his throat.

He could feel the life flowing from his body. The world was growing dark, and he felt as cold as he had ever felt before. His last thought was of his family.

"Run!" he prayed, "Run to the forest …"

And then … nothing.

.     .     .

Now he was hearing the hounds again. He wanted to ignore their baying, because it was winter and he needed to sleep, for he was now Barbuk, the king of the bears.

However, the baying wouldn't be ignored. Instead it grew closer and closer, until it came from directly outside his den.

Enraged, he roused himself, and stormed out to meet those who had dared to disturb his sleep.

All around him there were snapping angry jaws. Who were these puny hounds to invade his territory? He would make them pay for their insolence.

He took a mighty swipe at the nearest hound, but the dog was quick and agile, and he was weak from hunger. Every time he tried to swat one of the loathsome mongrels away, somehow, they always managed to dodge out of harm's reach, before darting back in again with their snapping jaws.

He felt a pain deep in his side, and there he was again: King Harold, the ruler of the Great Kingdom. He held a heavy spear in his hands, and even while he, Barbuk, tried to swipe this insolent upstart from the land of the living, a cursed hound sank his teeth into his forepaw.

He roared his anger, momentarily distracted, then felt the spear stab deep into his chest, finding his heart.

The world was spinning ... spinning. He felt himself fall. He tried to fight, but his limbs refused to answer. He tried to roar but could produce nothing more than a feeble groan.

Before everything went black, he was aware that he, Barbuk, the mightiest of bears, must suffer a dog to tear out his throat ...

·   ·   ·

The room was spinning ... slower ... slower ... and ever slower. Finally, it stopped.

Harold was unaware that he had fallen to his

knees, his arms hanging, useless, at his sides. He bowed his head, and wept.

"No more," he begged, "Please, no more."

The effect of the ordeal – of seeing his own face, cold and heartless, through the eyes of his victims had been devastating. Had that laughing, cruel man really been himself?

Harold had been given a mirror to look into, larger than the one his people held up for him to see, and he quailed before it.

Surely, it could not be. How was it possible that such a laughing, cruel man could be himself? After all, he was 'good ol' Harry', the darling of his kingdom. How was it possible to reconcile one with the other?

Eyes still pouring fire and magic, Kit glared down at the wretch before him. He wanted him to suffer every death that he had ever caused. He wanted him to understand that, for Barbuk and Pendarch, and all the rest, their deaths had held no meaning.

There had never been a duel, or a battle, or a noble contest of any kind. Instead, there had been Life, and then there had been Life taken away, for no better reason than one man's selfish lust for blood.

Now the fire and the Power began to wane.

"It is enough," said the tired, old voice. "There has been too much suffering already." Then that, too, was gone.

Harold struggled to his feet. His guardsmen leapt forward to assist him, but he shook them off.

"Everything," he said, tears streaming into his beard, "take everything from the Great Hall, and bury it in consecrated ground."

"Your Highness?" one of them had the temerity to ask, his mouth agape, as were they all.

Harold rasped, "Curse you, Tom, do as you're told! Right now, right this instant. Take everything down, and bury it honourably and well."

Tom crashed to attention, and snapped a quivering salute. "Yes, sire!" Then turning and stamping out of the room, the rest of the guardsmen fell in behind him.

Harold called after him. "Consecrated ground, Tom! Remember that it has to be consecrated ground!"

The King turned to a corpulent old gentleman dressed in rich black robes with a heavy cross of gold suspended around the folds of his neck.

"I'll trouble you to go with them, Bishop," he said. "See that it's done right."

The holy man seemed about to argue, but then changed his mind. Perhaps there was something in the king's eyes that he had never seen before, telling him that arguing would not have been wise.

"Certainly, Your Highness," and after but a moment's hesitation, he followed the guardsmen out into the Great Hall.

Harold turned, addressing the room at large.

"My Lords and Ladies, my honoured guests, I give you my thanks for coming this most special of nights," he glanced over at his daughter, and she smiled bravely back at him, "but now I must beg you all to leave."

There were several murmurs – some aghast, many resentful – but none that argued, and none that dared disobey.

"You too, Johnny," Mary called to the prince who still sat upon his chair, playing contentedly with a small wooden horse and knight. Amongst all of the assembled guests, absorbed in his own amusement, he alone had seen nothing of what had transpired.

Startled, he put aside his toy. "But shouldn't we set a date for the wedding, Mary-o?"

The Princess offered him a pitying look, and gave her head a slight, but definite, shake. "Oh Johnny," she said, "I've known you all my life, and if I should ever want to play Blind Man's Bluff, or Ring Around the Rosey again, you shall be the first I shall send for. But there will not be a wedding. At least," she glanced shyly at the young man, whose arm she still grasped to her bosom, "not one between you and I."

Prince John rose to his feet, hovered uncertainly for a moment, then smiled his relief. "I'm so glad," he said, "I really don't think I'm ready for marriage, yet. But Mummsy, and Daddy … well … you know."

Then he walked hurriedly past, calling for his squire to bring his horse.

Now the Queen rose and approached the gathering, her mien severe.

Bravely, Mary placed herself between her young man, and the formidable queen. For the first time in her young life, her course was clear, and she would not be swayed.

She spoke, her voice low but clear. "If Love be a spell, Mother, then I submit to its bewitchment, and gladly."

Juliana favoured her daughter with the same iron will that had always succeeded in ruling both King and Princess in the past. Tonight was different, though, and she knew it. Even as she battled with her furiously blushing, but wilful child, she could see that, tonight, she had met her match.

"Wherever he goes, Mother, I too, shall go," then blushing more furiously than ever, she added, "if he will have me."

The queen studied Kit closely for a good long while in utter silence, and then, wonder of wonders, she smiled.

Perhaps there had been some lingering vestige of Power that she saw. Or perhaps what she sensed wasn't the magic, at all, or not magic in its accepted form. She looked deep into Kit's brave heart, and saw what nobility really was.

"Then, daughter," she said, never taking her eyes from the prince, "let your young man cast his spell, and let him know that it is with my blessing."

"I take it," she continued, but for the first time directly to the Prince of the Enchanted Forest, "that I shall have my husband back, at long last, and that he shall never more go a-hunting?"

"You may take it, Madam," quoth the King with a last vestige of royal dignity, "that you and I may *reacquaint* ourselves with one another. After that, we shall see. But, no," he agreed, "I shall never hunt again. Not only that, I vow that I shall outlaw this barbarity throughout the kingdom. On this I swear my most solemn vow."

Harold was coming to see that, the terrible reckoning that had been wreaked upon him, was a marvellous opportunity of reacquainting himself with the person that he felt he should have been all along.

Besides, he reasoned, if this was his daughter's free choice (as free as love ever is) he had to accept that he wasn't losing her, but gaining an enchanted prince, instead.

Juliana smiled indulgently, "Yes, dearest, perhaps we shall discuss this further in the garden." She glanced at the young couple, who were very much unaware of anyone else.

The King, as is the way of all men, was not quick to understand, but having caught on to the meaning of his wife's arched eyebrow, suddenly declared that a walk amongst the roses sounded like just the thing.

However he was still mistaken, for the Queen shook her head. Glancing meaningfully at the forest creatures huddled together at the buffet, she said, "I meant the vegetable garden, darling."

"Quite so, my dear," Harold agreed more quickly this time. Then to the companions, he called, "Well, how does that sound to you?"

As one, they looked uncertainly from him to their chief.

"It's all right," Kit told them, "you are safe here."

Still they hesitated.

Then, "Roots and Honey?"

Harold turned an inquiring eye to his

daughter's handsome young man.

"He wants to know if they can bring the food with them," Kit translated.

Harold frowned, "You can speak with these forest creatures?"

"Sire," he gravely replied, "I *am* a forest creature."

"Yes," the King nodded thoughtfully, then he smiled, "yes, I suppose you are." He pulled a bell-pull, and Smithers appeared on the instant. Instructions were given, and in a trice, an army of servants had arrived to transport the larder to the garden.

When they had gone, with all of the food in tow, the companions, along with the King and his Queen followed close upon their heels.

Alone at last, the young couple continued to gaze deeply into one another's eyes.

"Please, Prince," Mary gestured toward the chair that would hold her future husband, "come sit with me."

Soon they were so ensconced, and once more gazing with the wonder of ancient recognition, each deep into the soul of their chosen mate.

They smiled.

Then they giggled.

.   .   .

There had been a final gathering of the companions.

"I cannot pretend to understand," Kit told his friends, his voice tight with emotion, "the magic, or the Power that has driven us on our quest, but I do sense that none of it could have succeeded without you," his eyes met those of each and every one, "you band of heroes."

"It wasn't like we had a choice," Gort scowled, but he looked pleased … for a badger.

Orso scooped up the little mouse, and perched him on his snout. By now he had learned to shut one eye so that he could focus with the other.

"Roots and Honey," he said. "Before, it was Big Bad. Then, you came, Mousey, and now all is Roots and Honey."

"No Orso," Kit said. "I was just an instrument; we all were. Everyone of us is roots and honey, including you."

Never one for the finer details, the bear shrugged. He had his truth, and it was good enough for him.

"I'm not bashful anymore," said Amos.

Unafraid, Lulu proclaimed proudly, "And I love how I smell."

"It was dangerous," Bumper allowed, "but we made it."

"We're all friends," Rowena said, her eyes glowing softly.

"*Best* friends," Chaser agreed, smiling.

Orso broke into his huge, good natured grin. The deer, porcupine, skunk, hare, and fox beamed back at him.

Then everyone turned to Gort.

The badger hesitated, but gradually, his lips managed to creak into a snarly grin.

"We are more than the best of friends," Tod said, perhaps summing it up better than anyone, "we are family.

And for that one last time, they were.

. . .

Kit and Princess Mary were married the very next day. As a result, the Enchanted Forest was united with the Great Kingdom and so, came under its protection.

For a honeymoon, they and the companions returned to the forest with a long baggage train of provisions for all of those who had had to do with so little for so long.

As they approached the border between the two lands, they could see that the first delicate shoots of green grass were already starting to grow through the ashes.

When they drew nearer, sprigs of green saplings could be seen sprouting from deep roots where there once had been trees.

The moment they crossed the border, the strong magic of Earth, Wind, Fire and Water once more combined to transform both Mary and Kit into mice.

"Do you think your mother will like me?"

Mary squeaked apprehensively.

"Why don't you ask her yourself?" Kit replied, directing her to a little old mouse who had just emerged from a nest burrowed under the roots of what had once been a mighty oak.

The little old mouse stared and stared at these strangers, scarcely believing her eyes. Then, overcome with excitement, she called into the nest before turning back and began to hobble as fast as her little old legs could carry her, towards her youngest, and littlest son … and his lovely new bride.

Behind her, the entrance to the nest was suddenly crammed with his siblings, each vying with the other to be the first to greet their brother home from his grand adventure. When they beheld their new sister, their joy knew no bounds.

There we will leave them, to enjoy the freedom that had been so arduously striven for. None were more deserving.

As for the rest, in time, the forest returned to itself, and so too, did those who dwelt there. For the balance had been returned to the land, and with it, their freedom to live as they always had. Neither god nor man would ever interfere with that again.

True to his word, King Harold gave up hunting for well and good. Instead, his huntsmen and hounds became wardens that policed the kingdom, ever on the lookout for those who would transgress the law.

The creatures that returned to the land came to

be friends with their fellow creatures who had stayed to husband it. With that mutual understanding, nothing more was spoken of demons, or fear of what was not known.

.   .   .

Finally, twice every year, on the summer solstice, and the Yuletide Festival, Smithers rode out in the Royal Carriage, into the heart of the Enchanted Forest, to where a young, proud oak had sprung from ancient roots. Here it was that he gathered the little mice that came out to greet him, and every year, that number grew.

Upon their return to the palace, the carriage would deposit, not mice, but Prince and Princess, and all their growing horde of gaily raucous children.

Harold had never regretted giving up the hunt, and with these visits, it was doubly so. For now, he and his queen had ample time to devote to each and every one of their grandlings, as they scampered, and scurried, with boundless energy, throughout their home.

Little mice, all.

## THE END

# Biography

CW Lovatt is better known for his works of historical fiction – the bestselling Charlie Smithers collection, and the critically acclaimed Josiah Stubb novels. "The Little Mouse" is his first foray into children's literature.

Lightning Source UK Ltd.
Milton Keynes UK
UKHW02f1408310518
323502UK00006B/27/P